The Copper House

JENNIFER A.
MOORE

2nd Book in the Waterdogs Series

Ark House Press
PO Box 163
North Sydney, NSW 2059
Telephone: (02) 8437 3541 ; Facsimile (02) 9999 2053
International: +612 8437 3541 ; Facsimile +612 9999 2053

All scripture quotations are taken from the New International Version,
published by
International Bible Society, 1984.

ISBN 0 9752044 7 5

Cataloguing in publication data:

Moore, Jennifer, 1968- .
The copper house.

I. Title. (Series : Moore, Jennifer, 1968- Waterdogs ;
bk. 2).

A823.4

Cover design and text layout: Nick Goodger & Nicole Danswan

This book is dedicated to
My Mother and my Sister,
whose love has been unfailing

and
Nan and Pop
who shared with me their memories of the copper house.

With special thanks to Wendy, who has encouraged me to write since the day we met.

Chapter One

Mikaela heard the plane before she saw it, the distant whine of the engine cutting into the summer afternoon haze. As she pulled the last of her dry washing from the line, her eye caught the sun flashing off the wings of the light aircraft as it banked, low in the sky. She watched it as it flew gradually around the country town, red stripe down its side, single propeller buzzing at its nose, then it leveled and continued north. The whining engine began to fade, but as it did, Mikaela felt a strange nervousness in the pit of her stomach and a sudden shiver stole across the back of her neck. She pulled the clean washing closer to her chest and breathed deeply, closing her eyes. It was just a plane…

'Hello, dreamer,' came a gentle voice from behind her, startling her back to reality. Two strong hands encircled her waist and she let herself lean back into the strong, safe arms of her fiancé.

'What were you thinking about? You didn't even hear me come into the backyard.'

Mikaela turned and smiled up at Thomas, breathing in his icy blue eyes and tangled sandy-coloured hair. He still took her breath away. She ran a finger across his cheek, feeling the years of farm work beneath the skin.

'I was just imagining our wedding day,' she sighed. 'The flowers, the music, the handsome bridegroom waiting for me at the end of the aisle…'

'I hope I polish up alright on the day.' He smiled at her, gently lifting back a dark strand of hair from her face.

She grinned at him as she placed her washing into the cane basket on the ground near their feet, then slipped her arms around his waist and drew close.

'I wouldn't care if you wore your greasy old overalls, Thomas McDowell.'

'Watch it, I might just take you up on that.'

He kissed her lips softly and then pulled away, producing something from the pocket of his shirt.

'Almost forgot to show you these. Terry from the jeweller brought them over this morning.'

He opened the small black box. Inside lay two gold wedding bands, glinting in the late afternoon light. Mikaela caught her breath as a wave of reality washed over her, and she fingered the diamond solitaire on her left hand.

'This is really going to happen, isn't it?' she breathed, hardly daring to take her eyes off the precious rings in case they vanished in a dream.

'You're not having second thoughts, are you?'

'Oh no, Thomas, never. I just can't believe how blessed I am to have such a wonderful man to marry. And I can't believe you want to marry me. Sometimes that alone is just so….'

'Unbelievable?'

Mikaela nodded.

'Thanks. It must be getting late.'

Thomas drew her to him and kissed the top of her head.

'I like a woman who has a way with words. You know, Easter's only two months away. There's a fair bit to do before we get all mushy about the wedding day.'

'Did you know that I'm going to wear your mother's bonnet?'

Thomas chuckled low in his throat and nodded.

'Yes, I heard about that. I hope she didn't force you into wearing it. She's a bit sentimental about that hat.'

'She didn't force me at all. And it's a bonnet, Thomas, not a hat. Apparently if you are an Easter bride, you can wear a bonnet.'

'Well, I wouldn't care if you turned up in a ute bonnet. I'd still marry you.'

'A ute bonnet, now there's a thought…'

She saw him glance suddenly at the horizon and smiled to herself. The sky was his clock. It didn't matter how long she spent with him, she would never understand all he could read from the sky.

'We'd better get going if we want to be at the Scott's for tea. I'll take this lot inside.'

He lifted the washing basket from the ground and lugged it across the small backyard. Mikaela lingered, noting his strong back and broad shoulders. Thomas was right - so many things had to be done before the wedding, and yet all Mikaela really longed for was to be able to make a home with this man. Then there would be no need for goodbyes.

She closed the lid of the peg bucket and turned to follow, but came to a halt when she noticed the sound of the aircraft engine. Slowly turning her head, she spotted the plane again, still a long way off but becoming larger in the sky. The sun was very low behind her, stretching long eerie shadows across the yard. A chill spun up her legs and into her spine, despite the heat of the late afternoon. The plane banked slightly and she watched it fly around to the east of the town, above the silos. Then it turned again and this time came directly towards the house.

As if in a nightmare, the back door seemed miles away, and her legs would not move fast enough. She scrambled across the grass, aware of the noise becoming louder with every desperate step. Then suddenly she was on the verandah and stumbling through the fly wire screen. Thomas had placed the washing basket on the kitchen table and now turned to her with wide eyes.

'What's the matter? You look like you've seen a ghost.'

Mikaela leaned against the closed door for a moment and took a deep breath, trying to gather her thoughts. A thin line of perspiration trickled down the centre of her back. Outside she was dimly aware of the drone of the plane as it continued south.

'I'm fine,' she managed, 'I just tripped up the back step.'

'We should fix that one day, before someone breaks their leg.'

'I'm just clumsy.' She pushed her dark braid away from her shoulder and breathed deeply. Her heart began to steady in her chest and she tried to conceal her subsiding panic from Thomas. 'Shall we go?'

'Sure.'

She took her handbag from the bench and then turned to close and lock the back door, aware of Thomas' eyes on her.

'Are you sure you're okay?'

'Yes, Thomas,' and she took his hand and squeezed it, smiling into his face. As they walked through the hallway to the front door, she knew why he was concerned. She had never locked her back door before, not in this sleepy country town. So why was she doing it now?

Chapter Two

As the red ute cruised north along the Henty Highway towards Andy Scott's house, Mikaela took a moment to reflect. Turramore was only a small Mallee town, but during her year working as a teacher, Mikaela had come to love the environment and the relaxed country feel of the place. She adored her modest teacher's residence, took great pleasure in her class of young children and was starting to feel at home with the people who lived in the area. The calendar of farm life was beginning to make sense – there was a time for preparing the ground, a time for cropping, for spraying the crops and then harvesting them at the end of the year. Then there was a multitude of other jobs in between, just to keep properties maintained. Fences were fixed, sheep were sheared and shifted between paddocks, machinery was greased, grain was loaded into the silos…

The silos – originally they had been fascinating, standing tall and majestic on the other side of the highway. They were huge, towering into the sky, watching over Turramore.

Then Andy had fallen from the top of one, plummeting to the ground and consequently losing all movement and feeling in his legs. He had been wheelchair bound ever since, and though he remained cheerful, Mikaela sometimes caught a haunted look on his face as he watched his friends playing football or cricket down the street. Since that day, the silos had become remote and impersonal to Mikaela – symbols of objects that have no feelings and do not grieve for others whose lives have fallen apart.

Andy was not one to give up, however, and Mikaela took joy in that. He had joined a basketball team for people in wheelchairs that met in Hillsford and he had taken on a great- er role working at the bank in Leighton where his father was the manager. Andy was a survivor.

Andy was also her cousin. She smiled to herself as she remembered his face when she had explained it to him. His jaw had nearly hit the floor, but she could tell he was exuber- ant. He had begun to treat her differently, to open up to her more, as if she was a sister. His mother Elizabeth had done the same, and it was a strange but happy feeling to have a sense of responsibility to these people who a year ago had been total strangers.

Then there was Gareth, dear strange Gareth with his funny cranky ways and his brilliant teaching skills. She had spent a lot of time with Gareth during the summer holidays, gradu- ally getting to know the man who had fathered her and then emotionally and physically detached himself from her moth- er. Every day was another step towards an understanding between them, a growth of relationship. It was hard work in some ways, but it was wonderful and thrilling – it was a God thing.

'Earth calling Mikaela.'

She turned to look at Thomas, taking a while to actually see him through the fog of her thoughts. Music was playing on the radio, the air conditioner was pumping out on full blast – she hadn't noticed any of it.

'You're not really here this evening, are you City Girl?' Brilliant blue eyes twinkled from beneath his creased brow.

'Sorry,' and she laughed and grabbed Thomas' arm. 'I was just reliving the last year. So much has happened, sometimes you don't get a chance to just sit and think. It's refreshing.' She let herself sink deeper into the seat and gazed out through the window.

'A lot has happened,' Thomas agreed. 'I'm not sure how we survived it all.'

From the corner of her eye, Mikaela saw him rubbing absent-mindedly at a scar on his hand, and in her mind's eye she saw flames.

'I know how. God gives us the strength to be survivors, in all kinds of ways. Maybe last year was a year we just had to get through.'

'You've got to survive being married to me yet,' grinned Thomas. 'That might be even more difficult.'

'Possibly,' Mikaela replied, 'but it's got its benefits…' Thomas responded with a wink and she grinned at him.

They were quiet for a while, watching the brown land go by on either side, worked over and ready for sowing after Easter. Something caught her eye, and when she looked up, she saw a hawk drifting across the sky. She remembered the aircraft.

'I saw a small plane this afternoon,' she commented, still watching the bird. 'It seemed to be circling around the town. What would that be?'

'That would be a small plane circling around the town.'

'No, I mean, what was it doing?'

'Circling around the town.'

She gave a Thomas an exasperated look.

'You're right, this marriage is going to be tough.'

13

Thomas laughed heartily and patted her leg.

'Sorry, Mikaela girl. A small plane…it was probably one of the boys from Hillsford checking out the farm borders. They spray the crops later in the year for a few of the blokes around the district.'

'It had a red stripe and one propeller at the front.'

Thomas nodded.

'Yeah, that's the Piper Pawnee. I think old Max Reubin used to fly that one, but he's given the job away now. They've got a new bloke in, can't remember his name. Are you thinking of taking a joy flight?'

'Not in that. It looked pretty flimsy.'

'Flimsy but useful. Not sure if we'll get them in to do our crops this year or not…' Thomas disappeared into his own thoughts.

Mikaela nodded quietly, then gazed back out the window. The hawk had disappeared.

*****

The Scott's house was situated halfway between Turramore and Leighton, although the Scotts always insisted it was on the Turramore side of the border. It was a large sprawling affair that had been in the clan for generations, built for much larger families than the current Scotts, who consisted of two parents and one son. Ian Scott had sold off much of the original farmland as his own career took a different path and he became the manager of the bank in Leighton.

Thomas drove the ute up the long dirt driveway to where the house stood, surrounded by pepper trees and gums, and parked the vehicle along the fence. Summer was having a final fling, and Mikaela had forgotten how hot the evening was as they stepped out of the air-conditioned cabin. Flies hummed around and tried to sit in the corners of their eyes, looking for moisture. Thomas led Mikaela around to the back of the house as was the custom in the country – people rarely used the front door – and Elizabeth greeted them, drawing them into the cool interior of the living room where another air-conditioner was rumbling quietly.

'Thought you were never coming,' grinned Andy as he wheeled towards them and shook Thomas' hand. Mikaela lent down and kissed his cheek.

'Happy birthday, Andy,' she said. 'Sorry we're a bit late.'

'Parking, were you?'

'Andy, for goodness sake,' came Elizabeth's voice from the doorway. Andy grinned again, his blonde wispy locks framing his face in a boyish way. Eight months ago his hair had been shaved off and his head was criss-crossed with angry stitches. Now his hair had finally grown enough to cover the ugly lines.

'Present for you,' Thomas announced, bringing a nicely wrapped and obviously round object from behind his back.

'Thanks guys, you shouldn't have gone to the trouble.'

'No trouble. Hope you can make a few slam-dunks with that.'

Mikaela hit her fiancé on the arm.

'Thomas, you just told him it what it is!'

'He already knows – he picked it out himself.'

Andy unwrapped the gift and tossed the basketball high in the air.

'Mik, you don't know half of what your man does. He's a pretty cool bloke – 'on the ball', you might say.'

'Oh please, I think I'll go help your mother.' Mikaela left the two friends with their banter and went into the kitchen area where Elizabeth was chopping tomatoes. She was a tall thin woman with a constantly worried look around her eyes but a lovely smile. Now she pushed a thin blonde-grey strand of hair back into her clip as she turned to Mikaela.

'It's good to see you, honey. We're just having a cold tea

tonight. It's been such a hot day.'

'That sounds lovely. Where's Ian?'

Elizabeth tipped the chopped tomatoes into a large serving bowl and began to pull apart a lettuce.

'He's just putting the hoses on in the garden. You've got to keep the water up to the vegetables in this weather, or you end up losing the lot. Here he comes now.'

The back door shut with a bang and in came Andy's father, immediately filling up the house with his presence. He was as big as his wife was thin, his shirt buttons straining and his belt slipping below his bulging stomach. He grabbed Mikaela into a hug as he entered the kitchen, smelling of sweat and soil.

'How's my favourite niece tonight?' he chortled, squeezing out her breath. Like his wife and son, he had taken Mikaela in as one of the family.

'Fine thanks,' Mikaela squeaked.

'For goodness sake, Ian, let the poor girl go. She'll break a rib or something.'

Ian released her with a smile and gave his wife a quick kiss on the cheek.

'Isn't this nice to have all the family over for tea?'

Elizabeth smiled patiently at her husband and then looked at Mikaela with gentle eyes.

'It is nice, you know.'

'I'd better wash up before tea then. How's the school teaching going?'

His big voice became muffled as he disappeared into the laundry behind the kitchen.

'Fine,' Mikaela called.

'How's the old codger?' The laundry tap started and Mikaela could barely hear above the rushing sound of water.

'Gareth? He's great – starting up some new reading programs for the older kids.'

The water sound stopped suddenly and Ian re-emerged, drying his hands on a towel.

'A feeding program?'

'Reading, Ian, reading.' Elizabeth took the towel from her husband and hung it to dry on a hook near the door. 'Don't you ever stop thinking about your stomach?'

'No,' he replied and chuckled as he grabbed Mikaela's arm. 'Let's go and see what the boys are doing.'

'I thought I might help Elizabeth…'

'I'm fine, honey. Take that crazy man out of the kitchen for me.'

In the living room, they found Andy and Thomas in deep conversation about the cricket series. Mikaela settled into one of the well-worn armchairs and allowed herself a moment to relax, closing her eyes and smiling as she listened to the voices around her. She felt so much at home with the Scotts. When things became too daunting and unknown, she felt she could come here to this house to renew her mind and to gather strength. There was a cross-stitch hanging above the fireplace and she opened her eyes to look at it now. Elizabeth had worked on it during the long weeks that Andy was in hospital. She had told Mikaela that she felt her faith strengthen and grow with each stitch, even in the midst of despair. A great bird was taking off from a cliff, and there was a verse across its wings – 'Those who hope in the Lord will renew their strength. They will soar on wings like eagles; they will run and not grow weary, they will walk and not be faint.' Andy could no longer physically walk, but by the grace of God he was leaping into life with a spiritual strength Mikaela had never witnessed before. It was a strength that could only come from God, and which was nurtured in this home.

Elizabeth came in from the kitchen with salad and plates, stirring Mikaela from her thoughts.

'Tea's on, everyone,' she said as she placed the items on

the table. The three men and two women seated themselves comfortably around the table, and Ian led them in thanks for the food. Before he finished, Elizabeth added her own prayer.

'Thank you Jesus that we can celebrate our son's birthday...' She finished abruptly as tears threatened to overwhelm her.

'Amen,' finished Thomas and everyone opened their eyes and smiled at Andy before starting the meal. There was no need for more words.

Mikaela ate quietly and let the pungent aroma of pepper and vinegar fill her nostrils. Country people seemed to know how to make simple salads that were absolutely brimming with flavour. This was probably because the salad vegetables were all homegrown. Mikaela had discovered the joy of eating a homegrown tomato, compared with one bought at the shop. The tastes were incredibly different.

After a little while of relaxed chewing, Ian wiped the corners of his mouth with a serviette and nodded towards Thomas.

'So, how are the wedding plans coming along? Getting cold feet yet?'

'Fine and no,' Thomas answered, forking up some corned beef. 'Andy and David are getting fitted for their suits next week, the hall's booked for the reception...that's my side of the story.' He smiled cheekily at Mikaela. 'I think it might be a little more chaotic at your end.'

Mikaela nodded.

'Yes, well my dress isn't finished yet, the bridesmaids' dresses aren't finished yet, the lady who was going to do the cake pulled out yesterday because she's going overseas...' She broke into a grin, '...but who cares! We're getting married anyway.'

'That's the spirit!' encouraged Ian heartily, helping himself to more salad. 'There's too much fuss with weddings these days. I mean, it's not the day that matters, it's the life-time afterwards.'

'Who are your attendants again, honey?' asked Elizabeth.

'Thomas' sister Emily will be matron of honour, and my friend from school, Theresa, will be bridesmaid.'

Andy looked up from his meal.

'Ahh, Theresa - she sounds nice. Am I getting Theresa?'

Mikaela laughed.

'She'll be your partner, if that's what you mean.'

'Is she blonde?'

Mikaela gave a mock frown.

'Am I blonde?'

'No…'

'So what are you saying? That a girl is more attractive if she's blonde?'

Thomas chuckled.

'You'd better not get into this argument, Andy. You'll never win.'

Andy took a sip from his glass and looked straight at Mikaela with his dusty blue eyes. Mikaela caught herself thinking that he was still a very attractive man.

'I think you are ravishingly beautiful, Mikaela, and I am insanely jealous of Thomas for having you as his future wife.' A cheeky smile played at the corner of his mouth. 'So…is she blonde?'

Mikaela shook her head, smiling.

'She is, actually.' There was laughter all around. 'Happy now?'

'Very, thanks.'

Elizabeth began to gather up the empty dishes and rise from the table, but then appeared to change her mind. Mikaela saw her glance at Ian, and noticed nervousness in her look.

'Mikaela, I wanted to tell you something, and seeing as though we are all talking about the wedding, maybe now is the appropriate time.'

Mikaela glanced at Thomas and felt her face going red. Elizabeth continued.

'I think there's someone else coming to your wedding that you don't know about.'

Mikaela's heart quickened.

'There is?'

'Yes. My brother.'

The table fell silent. Mikaela had heard very little about Elizabeth's brother – her uncle. She knew that Elizabeth had been the first-born child, then Carolyn, Mikaela's natural mother, had arrived. Then at some stage much later there had been a boy, but he had headed north, leaving the farming life behind. No-one seemed to know anything about him – except Elizabeth.

'Your brother is coming to our wedding?'

'Yes, well…' Elizabeth breathed deeply, '...he's going to try to come. He may get here the day before, he may get here the day after. I really don't know. But I managed to get in touch with him and he wants to meet you.'

There were so many questions sitting on Mikaela's tongue that for a moment none would come out at all.

'Where is he living?' she finally managed. 'Gareth thought it was somewhere in Queensland.'

'No - Sydney. He's been there almost his whole life. He's…' she stopped, again glancing at Ian, who put his arm around her shoulder. 'He's…well…'

Mikaela waited, her heart beginning to pound in her chest. He was what? A millionaire? Sick? A murderer perhaps?

'He's what, Elizabeth?'

'Well, he's different. He's different, that's all.'

The answer answered nothing.

'Different?'

'But he's wonderful, so wonderful. And he adored Carolyn. He and Carolyn were the best of friends.'

Mikaela paused. Could she ask Elizabeth anything else, or was she going to get the same non-committal responses?

'Why did he leave Turramore?'

Elizabeth was silent long enough for Mikaela to realise that the whole subject was very tender.

'My mother and father thought it was best for him to go away.' Her voice suddenly cracked and her eyes became wet. Mikaela could almost see the memories floating back through her mind. 'They knew they couldn't provide properly for him on the farm. He needed more. And maybe there was a social stigma they found hard to deal with…'

'A stigma?'

'Like I said, he's different. But Carolyn loved him so, and she missed him a lot when he left. He was only ten years old.'

'Ten? He left home when he was ten?'

Elizabeth nodded, a tear falling across her cheek.

'I had married by then and left home. I hardly knew him.' Ian passed her his handkerchief and she wiped at her nose, sniffing. 'It would never happen nowadays. We would have done it all so differently. Mother and Father just didn't have the knowledge back then.'

During the discussion, Mikaela had been vaguely aware of Thomas' hand around hers. Now she felt a definite squeeze and turned to face him.

'Maybe we could talk about it some more another time?' he suggested. Mikaela looked back at the strain showing on Elizabeth's face and knew Thomas was right. As disappointed as she was, this was obviously something that needed to be teased out gradually and carefully from Elizabeth's past.

'I'll get the fruit salad, Mum,' Andy said cheerfully, and

wheeled himself deftly into the kitchen. Elizabeth dabbed at her eyes with the handkerchief, then she completed the task of collecting the dishes.

'I'm sorry, Mikaela. I get emotional so easily these days. You'll love William, I promise. I really hope he can make it down okay.'

So his name was William. The word bobbed around in Mikaela's head for a while as she listened to the clatter of plates and cutlery. William Farmer, the mysterious uncle she had never met, would be at her wedding.

She suddenly needed to speak to Gareth.

Chapter Three

Turramore Primary School stood squarely and solidly beside the Henty Highway. Flanked by gum trees, the brick building signified the importance of a good, firm education. Anyone who had grown up in Turramore or the surrounding district spent his or her primary school years inside its walls. Now Gareth Lewis and Mikaela had the vital task of imparting knowledge to the present generation of Turramore children.

Mikaela flicked at a leafy overhanging branch as she walked up the concrete path to the front door. For the first time in weeks there was a change in the morning – although the sun was bright, there was a fresh cold breeze that tried to get down the back of her collar. She pulled her folders and bag closer to her body and took a deep breath of the morning air. Autumn had arrived, which meant that her wedding day was not far away.

She pushed the heavy door open and clattered down the hallway to her classroom. Entering the room, she smiled to herself and felt a sense of peace and accomplishment. Her students' pictures and little stories were pasted across the walls and strung from the ceiling, creating colour and detail everywhere. She loved the children in her class, and they had proved themselves over and over in what they produced. This year she had a class of nine – two children in grade two, five in grade one, and twin girls starting their first year in prep who had already become a source of fascination for Mikaela.

She put her work on her desk, which was already piled with numerous stacks of activity sheets and folders, then checked the clock. She had half an hour before the first little feet would be running down the hall, so she left the room and went next door to the principal's class.

Gareth Lewis' room looked even more spectacular than hers. There were fish tanks and terrariums along the benches and posters of intricate diagrams across the walls, along with the beautiful work that his students had created. His class consisted of children from year three to year six, which was the last year before high school. The principal himself was this morning at a computer in the far corner of the room, furiously punching at the keyboard, his white hair sticking out in all directions. Mikaela came up behind him quietly and placed her hand on his shoulder.

'Is this nasty old computer annoying you again?'

Gareth turned to her and ripped off his glasses, then his fierce dark eyes softened and he smiled.

'I hate computers, Mikaela.'

'I know, but it's the way the world is going.' She sat down on a chair beside him. 'You know, you really shouldn't worry yourself about getting that computer program to work. Your students know more about computers than you do anyway – let them figure it out.'

'I think I'm just getting too old.'

'Never!' and Mikaela squeezed his arm. He smiled back at her, but she thought that this morning he did look older. She had imagined he could go on forever, teaching with that spark and spice that he always seemed to have, but of course this was not true. She shook the thoughts from her head.

'I spoke to Elizabeth the other day, and I wanted to tell you what she said. Have you got time now?'

The principal folded his glasses and placed them on the table.

'Anything to get me away from this blasted machine.'

Mikaela took a deep breath before she began.

'Well, she told me her brother wants to come to the wedding. I was pretty amazed, and then she didn't tell me any more about him. She obviously found it all very hard to talk about. Anyway, I was wondering if you knew anything.'

Gareth shook his head, his brows furrowing.

'Not really. I never knew him, and Carolyn never spoke of him to me. It was odd, now that I come to think of it. He was never at the house.'

'He was never at the house because he was sent away when he was ten years old.'

'Really?' Gareth raised his white brows. 'And Elizabeth knew this all along?'

'She's been keeping it all very secret, but I don't think it was her choice. I think her parents didn't want anyone to know anything.'

'So where does he live, this mystery man?'

'Sydney.'

Gareth leaned back in his chair, his large frame making it creak, and folded his arms. He gazed up at the ceiling with squinting eyes and frowned for a moment.

'Sydney…I remember Carolyn going to Sydney a few times when we were courting. She said she had friends up there, and I didn't think any more of it. Perhaps she was…'

'Visiting William,' finished Mikaela. 'She probably was. Elizabeth said they were very close when they were young. Maybe she kept up the contact.'

'You know where you might find the answers, don't you?'

Mikaela caught Gareth's stern look and nodded.

'I haven't been game to open it, Gareth.'

Not long after Mikaela had discovered that Gareth was her natural father, he had given her Carolyn Farmer's diary, the diary of her natural mother who had died after giving birth to her. It was precious, almost sacred, and yet intimidating at the same time, and she had let it sit in the bottom drawer of her dresser unopened.

'Why don't you have a read of it?' Gareth pressed. 'I never did, and maybe I should have.'

'I will…eventually.'

'You have a lot to discover, haven't you, Mikaela? How are you coping with all this new information?'

Mikaela sighed and glanced for a moment around the room. How was she coping? Sometimes it was like finding out little details about another person, witnessing the unfolding of a story, and then she would come to the realisation all over again that it was her own story. For Mikaela, adoption was a bit like finding lost puzzle pieces and then fitting them together without having seen the original picture.

'I think I'm okay, mostly,' she finally replied. 'It's exciting and new, sometimes a bit overwhelming…Mum and Dad have been great about it all.'

'Yes, I get to meet them at the wedding I suppose.'

'You'll love them, Gareth. Mum's an angel and Dad's as steady as a rock. They're looking forward to meeting you.'

'An angel and a rock – they sound wonderful, Mikaela,' and he patted her gently on the head, smiling. 'Your wedding day is going to be very special.'

'And rather different,' added Mikaela, 'with all these odd relatives walking around that I don't even know.'

Gareth chuckled and there was a sound at the door.

'Mr Lewis, we've got some moths for Gene Simmons.'

Gareth waved three older students into the room and they walked over to the terrarium.

Mikaela screwed up her nose.

'You called your blue tongue lizard Gene Simmons?'

'Because of his tongue.'

Mikaela looked at the principal in a daze for a moment, then shook her head.

'Maybe you are getting a bit old.'

'Cheeky…'

More students came into the room and the time for discussion was over.

'I'll see you at morning tea,' and Mikaela smiled at Gareth and left him to his class.

*****

That afternoon, Mikaela drove herself to Hillsford, a larger town south of Turramore. It was in Hillsford that the local communities shopped for clothing, furniture and gifts. Hillsford also had a bridal store that hired out suits, and it was here that she was hoping to find Thomas and his groomsmen.

Her ute rattled loudly down the highway, and she wondered if one day it might just fall apart all over the road. She had borrowed it from Thomas not long after she had arrived in Turramore, and it had been in fairly poor condition back then. She probably should have bought herself something a little more modern by now, but she had developed a soft spot for the rusty old machine. I'm starting to have feelings for my ute, she thought to herself. I need to get a life.

The sun was losing its heat rapidly by the time she arrived half an hour later, and the cold air nipped at her ears as she got out of the ute. Summer certainly didn't hang around for long in the Mallee. She spotted Thomas' red ute parked outside the bridal shop and a thrill went through her body. Thomas looked great in a suit. He'd been a groomsman at his sister's wedding the previous year, and seeing him dressed up had taken Mikaela's breath away. Soon he would be standing at the end of the church aisle in a suit fitted for his own wedding, and Mikaela couldn't wait.

She pushed through the door, making it jangle, then stepped into the small store. Andy and David were seated beside the window and looked up when she entered.

'Hey, Mikaela, how are you?' David asked, smiling in his gentle way. 'I wasn't sure if you'd make it down here today.' His dark hair had been combed neatly and he looked relaxed.

'I wouldn't miss this for the world,' she said, taking a seat near Andy's wheelchair. 'Besides, I wanted to make sure you guys knew which suits to order.'

'Thomas knew just what to look for,' said Andy. 'And unfortunately you've missed the fashion parade, because Dave and I are already done. But Thomas, on the other hand…'

Before he could finish, a curtain drew back from a dressing room on the other side of the shop. Mikaela's eyes flicked across the room and Thomas was there, dressed in a black suit with a white shirt and a deep green cummerbund. He hadn't noticed her yet and was looking down, fiddling with the hem of the coat.

'I'm not sure if it's too long …' he began. Andy cleared his throat.

'Um, lover boy, your lady arriveth.'

Thomas looked up to see Mikaela, his blue eyes meeting hers in a rush, and she smiled at him, lost for words. He looked so smart and handsome, and the suit fitted him perfectly, sitting smoothly over his broad shoulders. He seemed taller and quite stately, just like a prince. She shook her head – she was making it sound like some fairytale she would read to the children in her class. But she couldn't help it – he did look like a prince.

'What do you think? Is it alright?'

It took a moment before Mikaela realised that Thomas was speaking to her. Her voice caught in her throat.

'Um…it looks…great.'

Thomas raised his eyebrows.

'You don't sound too sure. Maybe it's not the right fit.'

'No, Thomas, it's great. You look really…great.'

'I think the lady's lost for words,' piped up Andy. 'You'd better get over here before she faints.'

'I'm fine, thank you Andy,' Mikaela laughed, elbowing her cousin gently. 'I'm just not used to seeing any of you blokes all dressed up like this. It's a bit odd.'

'Okay, so now I'm odd.' Thomas pulled at a sleeve. 'What about we look at another style…?'

Mikaela got up from her seat and walked over to where Thomas was standing. Taking his hand, she leaned forward and whispered into his ear.

'I love you, Thomas McDowell, and you look so good I could marry you right here.' She smiled to herself as she saw the colour rise in his face.

'Hello! Earth calling the lovebirds! Can we go home now?' Andy's voice reached them from the other side of the room.

Thomas broke away from Mikaela, clearing his throat.

'We can go home now, Andy. The boss is happy.' He squeezed Mikaela's hand and gave her a wink.

David and Andy left them to finish the payment details and to arrange the pick-up of the suits. Thomas changed back into his working clothes, and then he and Mikaela left the shop and meandered outside. The sun was stretching into a glorious pink sunset across the western sky, and casually they made their way towards the nature reserve that flanked the Yarriambiack creek at the edge of town. The creek here in Hillsford was the same one that ran along the edge of Turramore, but here it was wider and more picturesque. An arched wooden bridge spanned its widest part, and Thomas and Mikaela walked slowly across it, hand in hand.

Mikaela breathed in the country air, the stillness, the peace of the early evening, and marveled again at the fact that she was holding the hand of the man with whom she would spend the rest of her life.

'It still amazes me, you know, how we met.'

Thomas smiled and looked thoughtful.

'If I remember correctly, you were looking at your reflection in the glass window of the store. I came along and saved you from your own vanity.'

'I was not looking at my reflection, you toad. I was wondering why the store was shut in the middle of the day. It doesn't happen much in the city, you know.'

'So I've been told. Hmm, 'toad'…that's a new one.' He grabbed her around the waist, squeezing her, and she giggled loudly.

'Watch out, I'll fall into the creek.'

'Who would be the toad then?'

They laughed together, leaning on the railing of the bridge, then paused to take in the watercolour painting of the sky, the blues and pinks running into each other over the fading sun. A bird skimmed the top of the water, catching insects, and a scarlet fish moved under the surface. Mikaela closed her eyes and felt a warmth surround her, the warmth of security and love and faith.

'We should pray, Thomas. We should thank God for everything we have, for each other.'

'I thank God for you everyday, Mikaela.'

She opened her eyes.

'You do?'

Thomas nodded, looking at her with serious blue eyes.

'You came into my life just when I thought there was no meaning anymore. I'm not sure where I'd be now if it hadn't been for you.'

Mikaela smiled and leaned her head against Thomas' shoulder.

'God's timing is perfect, Thomas. He knew we needed each other. He brought us together.'

She closed her eyes and began to pray, thanking God for Thomas, for their meeting and their engagement, their love and their future together. Thomas prayed too, his words brief but sincere, and when they were finished and they opened their eyes, the sky had deepened to a rich crimson, spilling over the distant horizon and reflecting in the waters of the creek.

'It's God saying thank you,' Mikaela whispered, and they stood silently for a while in awe of the beauty of nature.

Finally Mikaela glanced at her watch and stretched her arms lazily.

'I could stay here all night, but lesson plans call. I still have two days of teaching before the weekend.'

'It's been good to get away for a bit,' Thomas said as they walked back across the bridge towards the main part of town. 'Sometimes I get so caught up with life on the farm, and you get so busy at the school, we forget to spend time like this.'

Mikaela nodded in agreement.

'And that can happen even after people get married. We must try to take time out occasionally, time to refocus.'

They reached Mikaela's ute. The bridal shop had closed for the day, the lights off and the windows shut. Thomas took Mikaela in his arms and held her close.

'Soon we won't have to say goodbye anymore. I'm looking forward to that.'

Mikaela smiled and sighed.

'That is exactly what I'm looking forward to, Thomas Mc-Dowell.' She kissed him deeply and they lingered for a moment more before she got into the ute and turned the ignition. Waving one last time, she headed for home.

*****

That night, clad in her dressing gown and holding a cup of warm milk, she pulled out the bottom drawer of her dresser and found the battered brown leather diary that had belonged to Carolyn Farmer. She gently fingered the cover, tracing the worn stitching around the edge, then after a moment more of reverent stillness, she pulled off the rubbers bands and carefully opened the book.

The pages inside were intact but yellowed and slightly brittle. The writing was large and looped, and ran smoothly over the lines in a relaxed manner. Mikaela flicked through the pages. The entries were not daily – in fact most were separated by weeks and even months, all in the same rounded hand, mostly in blue ink. She touched the paper gently, seeing words here and there as her eyes skimmed the pages – 'cropping', 'sunshine', 'dust' – pages describing life on the land through the eyes of a young woman.

She came across Gareth's name and read the entry.

Sept 6th, '73
Spent today at home with the flu. Hardly have the energy to write, but must tell you what my sweetheart Gareth did. He arrived after dinner with a bag of lemons, and a bunch of yellow roses. Then he made me a hot lemon drink – it was so strong I could hardly drink it, but I did not tell him that! He is so wonderful to me. I can never imagine being with anyone else.

The entry finished, leaving Mikaela thoughtful. She knew how the story ended, how Gareth had turned his back on Carolyn when she needed him most. By reading this diary, would she begin to feel bitter towards Gareth? So far she had felt nothing but love and pity for the man. The fact that he had had a failed relationship with Carolyn had been something she had been able to observe as an outsider – she had been the product of that relationship, but had had nothing to do with the emotional scaffolding around it. Now that she was able to read Carolyn's deepest feelings about the man she had loved, it could be easy to blame Gareth all over again. Mikaela would have to remain objective and clear-headed – the time for bitterness and regret had passed.

She flicked through a few more pages. One day she would read it from cover to cover, one day when she had all the time in the world to soak in the stories from the past. Tonight she was searching for information. She skimmed over the pages, looking for William's name amongst the curved lettering. There were entries about the rains arriving, about a new dress Carolyn had bought for a party, about a tennis final she had just missed out on, but nothing about William. Mikaela's eyes were beginning to feel heavy and she was about to end her search when she came upon an entry further on in the diary.

March 31st, '75. Sydney

Billy seems a lot better this trip. Doctors have given him different meds, seems to be helping. He's made lots of friends and is happy in the house – the other fellows are nice to him. He says he loves me and he hugs me a lot, but he seems settled here and he doesn't want to come home with me. The medical people said it would be too much of an upheaval for him if I took him back home now. Mother and Father are in the nursing home and are so frail - it would probably be all too much for them as well.

I can still tell Billy anything and he just listens. He doesn't judge me. I love Billy so much, dear baby boy.

The entry finished, and Mikaela slowly closed the diary. Billy – surely that could only be William, the baby brother sent away from Carolyn at such an early age. The entry must have been written during one of her trips to Sydney to see him where he was settled in a house with some other people. Carolyn had been considering bringing him back to the farm, but it had been decided it would be best for him to remain in Sydney. There were still many gaps in the story, but one thing was obvious – Carolyn loved William very much. Maybe this was why he wanted to meet Mikaela, because Mikaela was Carolyn's offspring.

A cricket chirped outside and she stifled a yawn, suddenly feeling very tired. It was time to put the diary away. She would no doubt delve into its secrets again in the near future, but for now she was content to continue preparing for her wedding and to look forward to meeting William – 'Billy' – whoever he might be.

Chapter Four

The wedding was only three days away. Mikaela sat on an old petrol drum outside the Turramore general store, waiting for the V-Line bus that would arrive at any moment carrying the dearest people in her life – her family. Her parents and her two brothers were traveling north from Melbourne, along with two school friends including Theresa, who would be her bridesmaid. Most of her other guests would be arriving on the day of the wedding and leaving the following morning to return to Melbourne for work on Monday. The last few weeks had been a network of emails and phone-calls, organising travel arrangements, arranging last-minute dress alterations and finalising details of the reception. She had organised time off from work, and David, Emily and Andy had offered to run the youth group until further notice. At last, things were beginning to fall into place, and as Mikaela sat in the cool of the early evening, she felt she could breathe again, just for a moment. She had tried on her dress the previous evening and it was perfect. The florist was ready for Saturday, and the cake would be finished. It was time for organisational thoughts to take a back seat, and for family time to take over.

She smiled to herself as she watched a lone tumbleweed blow up the deserted main road. She used to think that tumbleweeds were only in Westerns. She had alighted from the same bus over a year ago, outside this very store. It had been hot and dusty that day, a typical summers day in the Mallee, and she had had no idea what she was getting into, coming to this tiny country town as a fresh young teacher. Who would have thought that just over a year later she would be getting ready for her own wedding? She shook her head, breathing in the crisp air and pulling her cardigan around her shoulders. Life was very unpredictable, but certainly full of happy surprises.

A noise from the end of the street alerted her, and a large passenger bus nosed in from the highway and slowly turned into the road. She stood, feeling a smile spread across her face. This was what weddings were all about – gathering together, loving each other, families meeting and mingling. Her heartbeat quickened as she realised with another rush how close the wedding was, then the bus pulled up beside her, braking with a jerk, and with a hiss the doors opened.

In a second, bodies were piling out and coming around her, her mother with her short, dark grey hair set neatly, her father, tall and thin, brothers, friends…she hugged them all, feeling tears prick behind her eyes, laughing and grinning and gasping.

'Oh my precious, it's so good to see you!' Her mother squeezed her tightly. Joyce Gordon was a little shorter than Mikaela, well-rounded, and full of cuddles. Mikaela pressed her cheek against her mother's soft curls.

'You too, Mum. I can't believe it's all finally happening.'

'Dad's got a really long speech ready,' said her younger

brother, Jeremy. He was an arts student, enjoying life at university without really worrying about where his study was headed. Mikaela sometimes envied his carefree attitude – nothing seemed to worry Jeremy.

'Yes, you'll be on your honeymoon before he's finished.' This was from Luke, older than Mikaela by three years, dark and brooding and settled into a career as a chemist with a pharmaceutical company. Luke was the serious member of the family.

Mikaela's father, Robert, pulled her to him.

'It's not that bad,' he laughed. 'I just wanted to tell everyone how beautiful my only daughter is.' He smiled, his cheekbones high and defined, his pale brown hair pasted down with something only fathers used. His coat smelled of the wardrobe in her parents' bedroom where Mikaela used to play hide-and-seek with her brothers. It was the smell of home and safety.

Theresa came up beside her, pecking her cheek, her long blonde hair falling gracefully over her shoulder.

'Hey, this is an interesting place you've chosen to get married in.'

'Yeah, does anyone else live here?' Mikaela's high-school friend, Erin, stood with her hands on her hips, staring down the road. She had short dark hair highlighted with copper streaks and wore black leather pants in Melbourne style.

'There's not many about now because the store's shut. But if you come out here tomorrow you'll be able to meet some of the locals.'

'I still think you should have got married in Melbourne. You know, in a big cathedral or something.' She sniffed with a look of disapproval and arched her eyebrow at Mikaela.

'Leave her alone, Erin.' Theresa smiled sweetly at Mikaela. 'She wanted a romantic country wedding. I would want the same if I married a country boy.'

'I'll remember to mention that to Andy,' Mikaela remarked, laughing at Theresa's confused look.

The wedding guests collected their luggage and followed Mikaela to her ute which was parked a little further down the road. Mikaela threw someone's bag into the tray and then noticed that the rest of the group was hesitating.

'Go on, just pile it all in there and I'll drive the luggage home. Then I'll come back and walk with you. It's not far.'

'You want us to put our stuff in there?' Erin asked, curling up her nose.

'It's fine, I swept it out this afternoon. It's just had an old dead sheep in it.'

'What?!'

'I'm kidding. Honestly, it's fine.' She smiled as she watched the passengers gingerly load their belongings into the tray of the ute. They remind me of me, she thought, when I first came to Turramore.

'How about I drive?' Jeremy's face was bright and eager. 'Then you can walk and catch up with the goss'.'

'You don't know where she lives, stupid,' Luke said casually.

'Well, she could tell me. It can't be hard to find.'

Mikaela patted Jeremy's arm.

'Thanks, Jeremy, but that wouldn't be the hard part. Driving the ute – that's the hard part.'

'It is?' asked her father.

'Well, it has no brakes, no shock absorbers and the lights are faulty...' She glanced at her father and caught his anxious look. 'But you don't need to hear all this.'

Grabbing him, she gave him a kiss on the cheek.

'Don't start worrying – just walk down this street until you get to the silos and turn right into Gladstone Street. I'll be walking back to you by then so I'll show you where to go from there.'

She gave her father another kiss, then climbed up into the ute and roared the engine into life. She spun the vehicle around in a dusty U-turn and chuckled to herself as she hurtled down the road towards home, leaving her family wide-eyed and open-mouthed behind her.

*****

The next few days flew by in a whirl of last-minute arrangements. The dresses and suits were picked up, the cake was delivered to the hall, the flowers were arranged in the church. Friends and relatives began arriving from all parts of the country and Mikaela spent time with each one, catching up on the past before she would be off and away again on her honeymoon. She began to feel quite distant from the one man she should have been spending more time getting to know, but she consoled herself with the fact that soon they would be together every day.

As the sun poked its rays through her window on the morning of the wedding, Mikaela stretched lazily in bed and felt a strong peace surround her. She could hear her family stirring in the other parts of the house, excited half-whispers, giggles, something dropping on the floor as suitcases were opened, but Mikaela felt at calm and at ease. It surprised her, this feeling of peace, but she knew without a doubt that it was God's message to her that what she was about to do was right and good. God had placed her and Thomas together for a reason, and their unity would be blessed. She closed her eyes and in the silence of her room dedicated this day and the rest of her days with Thomas to the glory of God, who had given each to the other.

The door to her room opened quietly and her mother entered, smiling.

'Hey Kaeli, are you awake?' She used the pet name she had called Mikaela since she was a baby. As she came across to sit on the bed, Mikaela propped herself up on the pillow and they embraced each other.

'I can't believe my little girl is getting married today – where have the years gone, baby?'

Mikaela rubbed her face into her mother's hair and closed her eyes, breathing in the familiar smell of her mother's shampoo and the scent of her skin. For a moment her eyes stung with tears but she swallowed down the lump in her throat and sighed audibly.

'Thanks, Mum, just for always being there for me.'

'I'll still be there for you, baby, even after you're married. I'll only ever be a phone-call away.'

They pulled apart slowly and her mother wiped at a tear that had strayed onto her face.

'Dad and I are looking forward to meeting Gareth today. I thought we might have bumped into him earlier, actually.'

'He's been busy. There's a relief teacher filling in for me while we're away on our honeymoon, and Gareth has been filling her in on school procedure.' She smiled to herself. 'That's his excuse, anyway. Personally I think he's nervous.'

'He has no need to be. We accept him already, as part of who you are and your history. It's important for you to know about your past, because one day you'll have children of your own and they'll want to know.'

'Children of my own…' repeated Mikaela. 'What a strange thought.'

'Let's get the wedding out of the way first,' winked her mother. 'I'll help you get ready.'

*****

It was now 11:15am. Mikaela stood on the porch of her little house, glancing down the street, her white satin A-line dress swishing around her ankles. She had adjusted the organdie from around her bridal bonnet so that it fell delicately down the back of her hair. Her locks had been pulled back into a French roll, with tiny pearl strings looping around the roll itself, and her make-up had been freshly completed. She was ready to be taken to her wedding. But her transport had not arrived.

From somewhere a lone crow was making throaty noises into the cold grey sky. Erin leaned over the patio railing and peered up the road.

'I knew things were meant to be slow in the country, but this is ridiculous. You'd expect the wedding cars to be here on time.'

'I don't know what could have happened,' Mikaela said, a small knot of nervousness tightening in her stomach. 'They knew the service was to start at 11am.'

Emily stood beside her. Her glossy auburn hair looked stunning against the deep blue that she and Mikaela had chosen for the bridesmaids' dresses. Now she put a hand on Mikaela's shoulder.

'Don't worry, they'll turn up. Eric's very reliable – there must be a good reason why the cars are late.'

As if on cue, the telephone in the hall rang. Mikaela heard the muffled sound of her mother's voice, then Joyce came out onto the patio in a rush, her pink pillbox hat sitting slightly askew.

'Kaeli, that was Mr Eric Porter. He was ringing from somebody's house. He said they had a problem with one of the vintage cars and it wouldn't go so they fixed it, but…'

'But?'

'Well, now they're all sitting behind a flock of sheep in a back road somewhere.' She smiled and shrugged helplessly.

'Terrific,' breathed Erin.

'Maybe you should have chosen cars that weren't so old,' Theresa offered from behind Mikaela's mother. 'I mean, I

41

know they belonged to Thomas' friends, but…'

'It wouldn't have made any difference if there are sheep on the road,' Mikaela replied. 'If there's a big mob of them, the cars could be stuck there for ages.'

'Who does things with sheep on a Saturday anyway?' Erin asked. 'Don't farmers have weekends off?'

'No, not if there's work to be done. And by the way, you don't 'do things' with sheep – you either shift them, draft them, shear them or crutch them.'

Erin raised one eyebrow.

'Crutch them? That sounds gross.'

'It means you take the wool off their backsides so they don't get flyblown, which is when flies get in and lay eggs and…' Mikaela stopped suddenly and put a hand on her hip. 'I can't believe I'm standing here in my wedding dress talking about flyblown sheep.'

'Neither can I, girl,' Erin remarked, shaking her head. 'Country life certainly has changed you.'

'What are we going to do about the cars?' Theresa asked. 'I mean, I'm sure this conversation is very stimulating, but I think we should move on to more pressing matters.'

Mikaela looked out over the street and then up at the sky, noticing grey clouds moving slowly over the sun. Rain had been forecast for later in the day. She took a moment more to think, then turned back to the others.

'I think we should walk.' She saw Erin start to say something, but before her friend could protest, Mikaela continued. 'Dad and the boys are already at the church because they took the ute. The rest of the town is at the church too and there's no mobile coverage here, so we can't ring anybody. It's not far up the road, so I say let's walk it.'

There was a moment's silence as the women looked at one another.

'You can't wear those shoes, baby,' Joyce said finally.

'Your feet will blister.'

'I'll put on my runners, and we can carry the good shoes with us. It won't be a problem.'

They hesitated for a moment more, and then Emily started to move.

'Well, come on everyone. You heard the bride – let's get a move on.'

The shoes were changed, and in two minutes all five ladies were walking gingerly down the road.

'This is so weird,' Erin muttered, pulling her fur-trimmed burgundy jacket closer to her body.

'You shouldn't complain,' Theresa said. 'It's not your wedding.'

'It really doesn't matter, everyone,' Mikaela sighed. 'It's not as if we're trekking to Mount Everest.'

'At least it's not a dirt road,' said Joyce, puffing slightly. Mikaela caught Emily's eye and they smiled at each other. A few seconds later they had rounded a corner onto the dirt track which was the short cut to the church.

'Well I could have guessed that was coming.' Erin rolled her eyes. 'Now we just have to wait for it to rain.'

Mikaela laughed quietly to herself. Erin had noticed the sky too. Rain was a distinct possibility.

The bridesmaids hitched their dresses up as far as they could go within the boundaries of modesty, and Erin and Joyce pulled up the skirt of Mikaela's dress to prevent dust from the road soiling the hem. Mallee dust is hard to escape, however, and Mikaela knew she would arrive at the church in a slightly off-white gown.

A little black and white fox terrier trotted from behind a house fence and gave a bark. After a moment of staring, it began to follow them, sniffing occasionally at their heels.

'Great, a party crasher.' Erin eyed the dog warily.

'That's Rupert. He's okay.' Mikaela smiled at the dog.

She was beginning to feel quite hot now, and she knew that the perspiration from her armpits had begun to soak into the tulle lace of her sleeves.

'Did anyone bring any perfume?' she asked rather breathlessly.

Before anyone could answer, a wet drop fell across Mikaela's face. She turned to her mother.

'Please tell me that wasn't a bird.'

Her mother shook her head.

'I can't see anything, Kaeli, but I...' Before she could finish, a few more drops fell and the source became obvious.

Erin glanced at the sky, squinting her eyes against the light rain.

'Okay, things are now officially bad.'

'Your hat, baby, and your hair...'

'Here, Mrs Gordon,' and Erin was taking off her jacket. 'You hold one side, I'll hold the other,' and they stretched the jacket over Mikaela's head as they continued to walk hurriedly.

'Erin, that's not good for your jacket,' puffed Mikaela.

'Forget the jacket. This is your big day.'

Up ahead they could see the little church. It looked beautiful in the misty rain, stained glass windows set in the stone walls and a large pepper tree at the front. There were a number of cars parked under the tree but the guests must have been seated inside the church. Mikaela could see two men hovering outside the door of the church, and she recognised one of them as Richard Rowe, the minister. The other was her own sweet father.

Emily and Theresa held their bouquets over their heads as they walked quickly and Joyce managed to shield herself with her clutch bag. It was at that moment that Mikaela heard Theresa give a gasp.

'Mikaela! Where's your bouquet?'

'Umm...' Mikaela kept walking, and after a moment's hesitation, so did the rest of the party. 'I think it's on top of the t.v.'

'You can use mine,' Emily said immediately. 'That is, after I've finished using it as an umbrella.'

'No, I'll give her mine-' began Theresa, but Mikaela interrupted her.

'I've got a better idea. Emily, pull up some of that for me.' She pointed to a group of yellow flowers that were growing beside the track.

'You know this is a weed, Mikaela,' Emily said, wrinkling her nose as she handed the plants to her future sister-in-law.

'I know, it's cape weed, and it's meant to be smelly too. Thomas told me about it one day when we were just getting to know each other. That was a special day, so these will be just perfect.'

Erin looked at Mikaela and shook her head.

'You're going to carry a weed down the aisle. Like I said, this is weird.'

In a few moments they had arrived at the church door and Richard bustled them into the entrance. There was a rush of explanation about the cars and Richard nodded and smiled sympathetically. Mikaela's father gave her a kiss.

'You're only half an hour late – don't worry.'

Theresa giggled and Erin rolled her eyes. Robert whispered into his daughter's ear.

'But you look absolutely beautiful.'

Erin and Richard took Mikaela's mother into the church through the glass doors. Emily dusted off Mikaela's dress as best she could and helped her to arrange the veiling from the bonnet over her face. The organ began playing from inside the church, and after giving the bride a kiss on the cheek, Emily and Theresa went through the opened doors and began to walk steadily down the aisle in time with the music.

Mikaela took a deep breath and put her arm through her father's.

'Are you ready?' He smiled down at her.

She nodded and together they moved into the church to follow the matron of honour and the bridesmaid. Faces turned to them as they began to walk down the aisle, people grinned, some reached out to pat Mikaela on the arm. She smiled back, feeling like she was now in a dream, a dream full of music and flowers and beautiful smiling people. For a moment she felt a sickening wave of reality wash over her as she remembered she was still wearing her runners. In an instant, heat prickled up from her neck and her heart began to beat rapidly. But at the same moment, she caught sight of Thomas ahead of her, standing and waiting, with David and Andy beside him. And in that moment all thoughts of her shoes, the cape weed, the dust and the rain vanished, and it was just Thomas who completely filled her thoughts. The suit looked even better on him than it had that day in the bridal shop. His light brown hair was golden in the pale light coming through the windows. His eyes were so blue, even from a distance, piercing her own with their honesty and commitment. And were those tears hovering at the corners? Her own eyes welled up with moisture as she drew closer to the man who owned her heart.

'Who gives this woman to be married to this man?' Richard was saying.

'I do,' her father replied solemnly, then he had embraced her and was gone, and Thomas' strong hands were holding hers. She looked up at him, her arms and legs trembling, but his intense gaze and sturdy hands gave her strength and she smiled. She saw his eyebrows rise as he noticed her bouquet and she laughed and relaxed slightly. The organist began the first hymn and as the congregation rose to sing, Mikaela allowed the peace of God to surround her and fill her. It was time to begin a new and wonderful chapter of her life.

*****

There was a clatter of plates and cutlery, and the sound of laughter from happy guests. Thomas was by her side as they moved between the tables, speaking to friends and relatives. A piano played in the background, a light rhythmic tune that danced around the people gathered in the Turramore Hall for the reception. Mikaela felt dreamy as she watched her surroundings – soon they would be leaving for their honeymoon and she wanted to remember as much as possible about the day. She could see Ian Scott laughing together with her mother, and her brother Luke in deep conversation with David. She saw her father and Gareth speaking closely at their table, and her father was smiling. She felt a surge of happiness and relief – these were people who were all so dear to her who were now all meeting together. It made the whole wedding even more special and wonderful. She felt Thomas take her hand and she turned to him.

'How are you going, Mrs McDowell?' he whispered in her ear, his breath warm on her face.

'I'm so happy. A bit tired I think, but very happy.' The sound of a lone glass being tapped by a spoon began, which gradually multiplied until every guest's glass had joined the tinkling.

'Well my love, that's our cue,' and Thomas leaned towards her and placed a lingering kiss on her lips. The guests clapped and cheered and Mikaela dropped her smiling face to hide the blush she could feel there. They had reached the table where some of her school and university friends were seated. Andy was mingling and causing mirth as usual – the sound of giggles floated up from the girls at the table. When Andy saw Mikaela, he spun his wheelchair around and came closer.

'Hey Mik, it's been a great wedding. Are you doing okay?'

'I'm doing really well, Andy. What about you? How's Theresa?'

'Theresa's great. But you know,' and he lowered his voice, 'I'm pretty impressed with the brunette.'

'Erin?'

'Yeah, she's really cool. What's her story – has she got a bloke already?'

Mikaela raised her eyebrows, the whole notion of Andy and Erin coming as a complete surprise. She stumbled on her words.

'Ah, no, I don't think so, but…'

'But what?'

'Well, Erin's…I don't know, she's just Erin.'

'She doesn't go for guys in wheelchairs?' It was Andy's turn to give the questioning look.

'No, I don't mean that. I don't know, maybe. Sorry Andy, you're making my words come out all wrong.'

Andy smiled and the atmosphere between them relaxed.

'That's okay. It happens with all the women.'

A delicate arm suddenly came around Mikaela's waist and the scent of roses touched the air. Helen, the mother of the groom, was looking resplendent in mint green silk.

'Hasn't it been a wonderful day?' she whispered into Mikaela's ear. 'You both look so beautiful together. It was all meant to be.'

Mikaela gave her new mother-in-law a kiss on the cheek and then Thomas was beside them both.

'I'm going to have to steal my new bride away from you, Mum. The band's playing 'Wish me luck'.'

'Looks like it's time to go, dear.'

'Already?' Mikaela asked. 'The day has just gone so quickly.'

The guests were already forming a large circle around the hall. Thomas led Mikaela to one side of the circle and they parted, each saying a special good-bye to the guests one by one. Mikaela gave her parents a hug while her mother burst into tears. She saw her brothers shaking Thomas' hand over at the other side of the circle. They had all met so briefly but they seemed be drawn to each other immediately. More friends hugged her, relatives were ready with kisses, and all the while the song played – 'Wish me luck as you wave me good-bye...' She bumped into Thomas half way around and he twirled her in a dance spin and kissed her forehead, causing more laughter and shouts from the crowd. She said good-bye to others in the circle and then she had reached the door, the door through which she and Thomas would walk any moment now towards their new life as a married couple.

'Mikaela!' Someone was pulling at her sleeve. The music and the singing were becoming louder and everything in her mind was beginning to whirl with the noise.

'Mikaela!' The voice was there again, loud and urgent. Mikaela turned to see Elizabeth, teary eyed but smiling in a strangely feverish way, perspiration dotting her flushed forehead.

'He's here! He's just arrived.'

'Pardon? Who's here?'

'William. He wants to see you.'

'But...' Her uncle. He hadn't been at the service and she had pushed her disappointed thoughts of him to the back of her mind, assuming he was not coming to Turramore at all. Now she was saying good-bye. How could her uncle turn up as she was about to leave? There would be no time to get to know him at all him.

'But I have to go...' She could hardly hear her own voice above the noise. 'How long is he staying?'

'Oh, he'll be here when you get back from your honeymoon. He's staying with us.'

Faces loomed in front of her then fell back, smiles, singing mouths, eyes, people patting her on the shoulder. Elizabeth disappeared for a moment then returned with the man who was William. Mikaela took a second to refocus.

He was quite short, a little shorter than Mikaela herself, with a lovely black three-piece suit stretched around a stout body. His greying hair had receded to reveal a bald patch on top of his head and he was wearing dark-rimmed glasses. The slanted eyes behind the glasses twinkled as his face creased up in a smile. He grabbed her hands in his own and Mikaela noticed how small and stubby they seemed.

'Lynny,' he said in a slightly muffled voice.

It took a moment for Mikaela to realise he was calling her the name of her natural mother.

'I'm Mikaela. It's nice to meet you.' There was a surge in the crowd and Mikaela could feel herself being pushed towards the door. 'I have to go, but I'll see you when we get back from Tasmania – okay?'

'I'm Bill,' came the reply. 'Goodbye Lynny,' and he smiled again and let go of her hands as she was herded out of the hall. Outside the cold air cleared her head, and as the throng spilled out onto the footpath to wave the couple good-bye, she realised what was different about her uncle.

William had Down Syndrome.

Chapter Five

The frosty wind whipped across Mikaela's face, making her eyes sting, and the smell of salt was strong in her nostrils as she stood on the bluff. She looked out over the water to 'The Nut', the strange tiny hill island emerging from the sea off the coast of Stanley. She could still taste the sweet John Dory she had had for dinner a short time ago. She knew the fish was fresh because she had chosen it herself from the tank, and then watched its preparation by the chef before it became her meal.

They had spent nine days in Tasmania, and tomorrow they would be leaving to return to Turramore. She had loved every moment on the island, soaking up the history and the character of the place. They had visited Cataract Gorge in Launceston, poked around the charming village of Evandale and sampled the sumptuous seafood of Bicheno. They had photographed the Ross and Richmond bridges, the rugged beauty of Cradle Mountain and the eerie stillness of the Port Arthur ruins. There had been lobster in Hobart and croissants for breakfast in Strahan, and fluffy scones with jam and cream while overlooking the strange glowing moonscape of Queenstown.

Now the honeymoon was almost over. Mikaela breathed in the sea air, watching the gulls wheeling around the Nut, and shivered involuntarily. Tomorrow they would head back to Melbourne, and then on to Turramore, where she would be Mrs McDowell, the farmer's wife…She smiled and shook her head. Who would have thought she would have become a farmer's wife? The term used to sound dull and lacking excitement, but she knew that a farmer's life was never really dull and there was probably a lot more to being the wife of one than people realised. Still, she remained nervous about her ability to cope with the responsibilities of McDowell Hill. The strange uneasiness bothered her and she tried to suppress it as she watched her husband return from his walk.

He smiled at her, his hair blowing crazily in the wind, and she saw him pull his thick sheepskin jacket closer around his neck. The fears subsided a little. Thomas would be with her every step of the way, and there was no need to assume she would have to deal with country life alone. He was strong and he was caring, and now that they were married he had shown her a gentleness she had never seen in him before. Their wedding night had been tender and fulfilling, because Thomas had made her feel relaxed and at ease with herself and their relationship. He was everything to her, and she knew that she was everything to Thomas. Their love would only continue to grow now that they had joined together in marriage.

Thomas reached her and took her in his arms, cuddling her close.

'Are you getting cold out here?'

'A bit,' she murmured, snuggling into his warm jacket. 'Better now that you're here.'

'We should make tracks back to the guesthouse. I don't know how many miles we've walked today, but it's going to get colder soon, and I'm looking forward to that fireplace.'

'Mmm, and snuggling under that feather doona with a mug of hot chocolate.'

'Forget the hot chocolate...' and he lifted her off the ground and spun her around, making her laugh. Hand in hand they began to walk quickly back to the road, breaking into a jog occasionally to keep warm.

'Thomas...'

'Yes?'

They puffed their way along the roadside as the air grew colder around them.

'You wont leave me when we get back to Turramore, will you?'

'Leave you? What do you mean?'

'It's been so wonderful here in Tassie, just the two of us to-gether. I don't want it to end. I don't want us to...change.'

Thomas squeezed her hand harder and laughed.

'You're a funny bird. You've got me for life, girl, and I'm not thinking of changing in any great hurry. So you'll just have to take me as I am.'

She smiled back at him and they laughed and ran, and Mikaela put all thoughts of returning home away for one more night.

*****

Thomas had been interested to hear about William. They had discussed the topic of Down Syndrome, and Mikaela had searched the recesses of her mind for memories of certain children with the condition whom she had taught during her teaching rounds. She had enjoyed working with them, and she had briefly studied their language and learning abilities, but there was a great deal she knew nothing about. She had never met an adult with Down Syndrome prior to William, and questions concerning life expectancy hovered at the edges of her mind.

She shook her head clear of the thoughts. She had been watching the Mallee trees go by, sunset orange touching their leaves. The glass of the car window was cold to touch – they would need to build a fire in the Coonara tonight to warm up the house. She looked across at Thomas, intent on the highway. They had had an accident along this part of the road the previous year.

'Looking forward to getting home?' she asked gently.

Thomas smiled and nodded.

'I am actually. They say you can take the boy out of the country, but you can't take the country out of the boy. I think I missed Turramore while we were away.'

Mikaela sighed quietly, and turned back to the window. Turramore was around the next bend. She watched the light play off the creek as it wound along towards the town. Just over a year ago she had watched the same creek from the window of a bus as she travelled to Turramore for the very first time, alone and frightened. This time, as they drove into town, she would belong.

The first thing she saw as they passed the Turramore signpost was Gareth's car pulled up outside the school.

'That man is a workaholic,' Mikaela muttered to herself. She wondered how he had got on with the replacement teacher, or rather how the replacement teacher had got on with Gareth.

They drove up the main street, which was totally deserted, past the general store and the post office, then turned left, heading westward.

'Where is everybody?' Mikaela asked. 'It's very quiet.'

'You've been in the big smoke too long, Mikaela girl. This is Turramore, remember?'

They headed out onto the Turramore West road for a while, the sun dropping below the horizon in front of them and needling their eyes. McDowell Hill eventually rose slightly on their right, its chimney showing among the gum trees, and Thomas turned the ute into the gates and down the dirt drive. They circled the enormous pepper tree and pulled up in front of the house.

A welcoming glow was coming from the lace-curtained bay windows.

'There's a light on inside,' Mikaela commented.

'I wouldn't be surprised if someone's set the fire too.'

They got out of the ute and pulled their luggage from the back.

'Welcome home,' Thomas smiled as they walked up to the front door. 'Leave your bags there – this is something I've always wanted to do.'

He hoisted Mikaela up with his strong arms, and pushing the front door open, carried her across the threshold, placing her gently down inside the front hall.

'That is so romantic of you, Thomas McDowell,' Mikaela laughed, giving him a close hug. 'But now we've got to go back outside and get the luggage.'

'Yes, I'd never quite figured that bit out.'

Laughing together, they pulled the remaining luggage inside and closed the door. The fire was indeed glowing peacefully in the Coonara, and Mikaela found that the fridge had been stocked with fresh milk, bread and vegetables. She slowly moved around the house as Thomas took their suitcases up the hallway, running her fingers over furniture and gazing into rooms. Thomas caught her leaning in the doorway of the bathroom.

'What are you doing, Mrs McDowell?'

'Oh, just soaking it all in.'

'The bathroom?'

'No, just the whole house. I live here now. It's a really strange feeling, but it's a wonderful feeling.'

'Mmm, I think I know what you mean. It's different for me too. I've been here so long by myself, and now that you're here the place feels warmer, friendlier...like a family.'

He slowly drew her to him, squeezing her gently, then looked into her face.

'I love you, Mikaela. Thank you for making Turramore your home.'

She melted into his blue eyes and felt his lips strong and increasingly urgent against hers. A heat rose up in her body and she allowed herself to be swept up in the passion of the moment.

Suddenly there was an awful sound from outside the tiny bathroom window, a siren wailing at full volume. Mikaela jumped so hard that she hit her head against the doorjamb. Thomas fell back from her, staring at the window, and at the same time a dozen other noises began – banging, clanging and rattling, people yelling. The noise was deafening.

'What's going on?' Mikaela yelled above the din, rubbing her head.

She saw a smile begin on Thomas' face.

'It's a tin kettling.'

'A what?'

'A tin kettling. The whole town's probably out there banging on old tins and boxes – it's a 'welcome to the district' sort of thing.'

'Well, I'm very glad they didn't leave it another twenty minutes,' murmured Mikaela, straightening her shirt.

'That has been known to happen...'

They made their way back out to the living room and opened the front door, to be greeted with the sight of at least thirty beaming townsfolk, armed with tins and sticks hooters and sirens. When the crowd saw the couple, they broke into a cheer, howling and clapping.

'Welcome home!' David yelled from the front of the group, and the crowd surged forward towards the verandah. Mikaela saw that people were holding plates of cakes and slices, and two others were carrying a large urn.

'Supper time,' said Thomas beside her, and they made way for the masses to enter the living room and spread themselves around on the lounge suite, chairs and floor. Two large men helped Andy up onto the verandah.

'Mrs McDowell, how are you tonight?' he asked as they brought him through the doorway and sat him in a chair.

'I'm…stunned,' Mikaela said loudly, over the din. 'Apparently this is a tradition in Turramore?'

'Absolutely. You can't escape from a tin kettling if you live in this part of the world.' He ruffled his hand through his fine blonde hair.

'But how did you know we'd arrived back? I mean, we'd told Helen we were coming back today, but we hadn't given her a time.'

'Spies. One spy, actually. He was posted at the entrance to town.'

Understanding came in a moment.

'Gareth. That old sneak. And I thought he was hard at work.'

'He rang through the message and we all got ready. He rang your closest neighbour too, and she got the fire going. Must have done that in a flying hurry.'

'My closest neighbour?'

'Just west of here – Mrs Hamilton. She didn't stay on for the tin kettling – keeps to herself pretty much.'

'I'll have to meet her one day…'

She was interrupted by Ian Scott pushing a lemon squash into her hand, and then she was pulled into the racket of her living room to socialise and meet people. She noticed Thomas at the far end of the room, looking happy and relaxed. It made her glad to see him like that, and she hoped in her heart that with the healing of his past and the beginning of this new chapter in his life, he would be able to be all that God had planned for him to be. She allowed herself to be drenched in the love and friendship of the townsfolk of Turramore while the party continued and it wasn't until the early hours of the morning that she found herself falling exhausted into bed beside Thomas and going straight to sleep.

Chapter Six

Mikaela's heavy eyelids gradually opened. The room was filled with light and sparrows were chirping outside the lace-curtained window. Memories and images from the evening before moved in her mind as she began to remember where she was.

Stretching and yawning, she turned over in the bed and put out her hand for Thomas, only to find an empty, cold space beside her. There were noises in the kitchen, so she struggled out of bed into the nippy air, donned her dressing gown and staggered down the hallway to the kitchen.

Thomas was dressed in his red flannel working shirt and worn jeans, and was standing next to the sink, sculling a coffee. He turned to see Mikaela and placed his cup on the draining board.

'Good morning, Mikaela,' and he took her gently into his arms and kissed her forehead. 'How was the first night in your new house?'

'Wonderful. Didn't get enough sleep though – what time

is it?'

'Almost nine. I've got to get out and check the air seeder.'

'This morning? You have to work today?'

'David told me last night that there's rain expected early next week.' He reached for his working cap. 'Once it rains, cropping will be underway good and proper. I've got to change the shears on the bar and replace some air seeder hose. And I better not forget to grease those nipples underneath the bin.'

'What…?'

'I'll explain later. I'll be home for dinner though – that's lunch.' He grinned and gave her a quick kiss on the lips. 'I love you,' and he was through the kitchen door and out onto the back porch. He stopped for a moment to call back to her. 'Oh, I've put the high tank on so you've got enough water to have a shower. It pumps water up from the low tank storage. Don't forget to turn it off before it overflows.' Then he was gone.

High tank, low tank – what was he on about? Rubbing her eyes in a sleepy daze, she turned back to the hallway to find her luggage and something to wear. A hot shower sounded very inviting. That would be the start of the first day in her new life as a married woman. She would try to forget that her new husband had gone off to work on the farm the first morning back from their honeymoon. She would push the awful thought that the farm may be more important to him than his new wife into the back of her mind.

It took her a while to unpack her bags and find appropriate clothing, packing away items at the same time into drawers and the large antique wardrobe that stood in the bedroom. Thomas' mother had left a number of antique pieces of furniture in the house when she had moved into town, all quite old and grand. Mikaela finished sorting her clothes, then headed down the hall to the bathroom, pulling a towel from the linen cupboard as she went. It was old too, but not in an 'antique' way. It was shabby around the edges and had a few large holes. Mikaela looked forward to opening some new towels that had been given to them as wedding gifts, and which were currently piled in one of the spare bedrooms with the other presents. This towel would do for now.

The bathroom in the McDowell house was very small and rather odd-looking. It had a bath, a toilet and a pale pink pedestal sink, all squeezed into a very tiny area. Because there was just no logistic possibility of fitting a shower into the room, Thomas' father had many years ago 'added' a fibreglass shower into the wall. The doorway of the shower was flush with the wall, while the back of the shower stuck straight out into the spare room behind the bathroom. It was actually possible for someone to knock on the back of the shower itself if the person inside needed to be hurried up.

Mikaela undressed quickly, the cold air biting at her skin. She was aware of a buzzy humming outside the window, and wondered if the noise was somehow connected to the high tank low tank thing that was meant to be on, and don't forget to turn it off, if you don't mind Mikaela darling, as I walk off through the door to work and leave you by yourself on your first day here…She shook the thoughts from her head. Get over it, Mikaela, she told herself. You sound like a spoilt brat.

She was now naked and she turned towards the strange shower entrance, but before she had time to ponder which way the door opened, a different noise began outside. This time it was the sound of rain, lots of it, coming hard onto the roof of the house and spilling over the gutters into the shrubbery outside.

'Rain's come early,' she said to herself. Early and strangely sudden. Very sudden. Realisation hit her. That wasn't rain – it was the high tank overflowing, and her precious shower and probably drinking water was gushing out all over the roof.

She grabbed the holey towel and flung it around her, then ran clumsily out of the bathroom, through the kitchen and outside. The freezing air knocked her so hard it took her breath away. She rounded the back of the house and saw a galvanized water tank sitting high up on a wooden stand, about level with the roof of the house. From it was gushing litres of water, splashing over the sides of the frame and down onto the ground in a rush of wastage. She ran over to the torrent, icy water hitting her like nails from all directions. There was a large old-fashioned light switch near the base of the stand and she quickly flicked it into the off position. The noise of the pump stopped and she was left with water trickling over the sides of the high tank until that too subsided. She stood for a moment, her feet bitterly cold in the muddy mess of the ground, her towel and hair wet and frosty. A breeze picked up and she began to shiver uncontrollably. Her heart was beating rapidly, but she felt a sense of exuberance - she had solved the problem. I'm okay, she thought, I can do this farm thing. Now it's time for a shower. She turned on her heels and hurried back around the corner of the house, her face turned down out of the wind.

'Streuth mate, look out!' A large round bearded man was standing in the path in front of her. She had almost run headlong into him.

'Oh my…I'm so sorry, I just had to turn off the high tank…it was running over, you see…'

The man looked her over for a brief second, worry edging his eyes.

'Er, you'd better get yourself inside, Miss. You look cold.'

'I am actually. Come in, I'll just…get some clothes on.'

She hastened inside, leaving her dazed visitor on the porch, then ran down the hall to the bedroom. Her mind was racing – who was the stranger outside and why was he at her house so early? She reminded herself that it wasn't really that early, but after all, this was the first day home after her honeymoon…the honeymoon that was slowly becoming a distant memory.

She threw on a pair of jeans and a chocolate-coloured jumper then hurried back down the hall. In the kitchen she found the hefty man standing rather awkwardly just inside the doorway. His beard was dark but neatly cut, and on his head he wore a grey cap that seemed way too small for the size of his skull. He was in his mid-thirties.

'I'm terribly sorry about that,' she smiled, holding out her hand. 'I'm Mikaela Gord – I mean, McDowell. I've only just moved into this house and the tank business outside just… threw me a bit.' She tried to smile again, but the man was still looking at her sideways.

'I'm Joey Boland, the fish man,' he said hesitantly. 'I come by every coupla months from Ballarat. Didn't knows there was a lady of the house here now.'

'Well, yes, there is and I'm her. Thomas didn't tell me you were coming today.'

'Oh, he would have forgotten, most like. Bachelors don't think of stuff like that.'

He poked a pudgy finger into his ear and began to absent-mindedly pick out wax.

'Last time I was here, he'd forgotten that he'd ordered two whopping bags of fertilizer from some bloke in town. The truck just dumped 'em at the front gate. I had to help him shift the lot into the old gardening room.' He studied the wax for a moment before flicking it away onto the floor. Mikaela felt her stomach turn. 'Anyway, seeing as I'm here and all, did you want some chicken?'

'Sorry?'

'I got good legs and breasts today.' He began to move outside and Mikaela followed in bemusement.

'I'm sure you have...' she began. 'Didn't you say you were the fish man?'

'Yep, that's right. Sell chicken bits and cheese - sometimes even fish. Blue grenadier mainly, but don't 'ave any today.'

His small white van was parked out the front of the house. Mikaela followed him around to the back and took a moment to inspect the goods inside the refrigerated compartment, eventually choosing a bag of chicken pieces. She scraped together enough cash from inside the house ('Don't 'ave no efposh rubbish out here' Joey had told her), and in another half an hour he had gone again, speeding back down the drive and leaving a puff of dust in his wake.

Mikaela stood there watching him go, holding her plastic bag of chicken and letting the silence envelope her once again. Joey would no doubt be visiting all the farmhouses in the district on his run. She shook her head in amazement. And won't he have a story to tell, she thought to herself - Thomas' new wife running around the yard on a chilly morning in a towel that barely covered her. The grapevine would be buzzing in Turramore by nightfall.

Suddenly she felt very alone. There was nobody anywhere and the silence around her was almost creepy. She hadn't achieved anything this morning, not even a shower. All she had managed to do was embarrass herself in front of the chicken/fish man. The moment of glory that she had experienced at the water tank was fading quickly. She was left with a huge unfamiliar house with nobody but herself in it, a huge equally unfamiliar yard which probably needed something done to it but who knew what, and a bag of withered-looking chicken pieces that didn't look like they would feed a mouse.

What do I do now? she thought. It was almost another fortnight before she returned to her teaching position at the school. Was she beginning to look forward to going back to work already?

Taking a deep breath, she turned to go back into the house, but as she did something caught her eye, something small and dark out in one of the paddocks to the north-east. She shielded her eyes with her hand and peered harder. It was a person, small and rather round, walking slowly and steadily, with a rocking motion as each foot hit the ground. A pair of glasses caught the sunlight and flashed brightly. It was William.

Mikaela ran inside to put the chicken pieces into the fridge, then came back out to greet her relative. She hurried across the front yard and out through the gate, meeting him as he climbed over the paddock fence.

'William! What are you doing here?'

'Bill, Bill,' he puffed, grabbing her hand. His face was covered in sweat and his long-sleeved white shirt was damp. He was wearing the long dark pants she had seen at the wedding. His eyes now crinkled into a smile. 'Good to see Lynny again. Good to see Lynny.'

'It's nice to see you too, but I'm not Lynny. I'm Mikaela.' The name did not seem to register with the man, so Mikaela took him by the arm and led him up slowly to the house. 'Would you like a drink, Will – I mean, Bill? Are you thirsty?'

'Mmm, Bill thirsty.'

'Have you walked all the way from Elizabeth's house?'

'Yes, yes, Lizzy's house.'

'That's a very long way.'

'Long way,' Bill agreed, and he allowed Mikaela to lead him up the front stairs and into the house. When they reached the kitchen, she pulled out a chair for him and opened the fridge, pouring him a large glass of water.

'This spiked, Lynny?' he asked as he took the glass from her. For a moment she was dumbstruck, then he guffawed loudly, his eyes cheeky and sparkling. She laughed with him, and sat down beside him at the table, watching him closely as he guzzled the water. It was hard to tell his age, even sitting here so close to him. His head was balding, and the remaining ring of hair was dark with flecks of grey. His skin was rather leathery and a bit wrinkly. She had done a few calculations while she had been away, and knew he must be in his mid-forties, possibly older.

'Lynny like the party?' he asked her suddenly, wrenching her from her thoughts.

'Yes, I had a great time. How come you weren't here, Bill?'

'Funny heart,' and he patted his chest solemnly. 'Get sick sometimes.'

'You have a funny heart? And you walked all that way this morning?'

'Walk everywhere, Lynny. No problem. Just funny heart, funny blood.'

He sipped again at his water, looking less like a beetroot now that he was cooling off.

'I'm glad you came to see me.' Mikaela felt herself beginning to fall under the spell of this man, who didn't seem to have a care in the world. 'Would you like me to show you my house?'

'Yes please Lynny,' and they got up from their seats. She let the name ride – for some reason she was Lynny to her uncle, and because he was happy with that, it worried her no further.

For the next hour they walked and talked. Mikaela showed Bill around the garden, the muddy tank stand, the orchard at the rear of the house, and the grapevine stretched across the front. As they walked, Bill pointed out plants and named them – lavender, cosmos, alyssum, and a funny furry-leafed little plant called lamb's tongue.

'How do you know all these names, Bill?'

'Lynny told me.' He looked at her suddenly, confusion over his face, and then it was gone and they continued to walk. As they did, Mikaela felt more and more comfortable with her uncle. He brought a simple happiness with him, and she could sense it in his voice and in his presence. His memory for plant names astounded her, and as he mentioned each name he seemed genuinely interested in each plant's well-being.

'This need more water,' he would say as they passed a drooping specimen. 'This one too. This one look like Granny Green's knees!' Then he would laugh out loud and giggle to himself for the next minute, leaving Mikaela smiling at his mirth and enjoyment of life.

They completed the circuit of the house and came around to the back door.

'There's the laundry, Bill. And after we've looked at that, we'll be just about finished.'

The laundry was separate from the house by a few yards, in its own little brick building with white trimming which Mikaela thought was rather quaint. There were two other rooms in the small building – one was known as the 'separator room', although now it just held firewood and odds and ends, and the other room was full of gardening tools and fertilizer. The fertilizer was what Joey Boland must have helped Thomas' shift a number of months ago.

It was while they were in the gardening room that Mikaela noticed an extra door set into the wall. It had a very small doorknob, unlike the other doors in the laundry block, and it had a keyhole with a small narrow key poking out.

'That's odd. I wonder where that door leads.' They stood in front of it for a moment, then Mikaela turned the key and pulled the door open. It was stiff from disuse, and the small doorknob rattled in her hand as she pulled, but she managed to drag the door open enough to reveal steps that descended into darkness.

'Cellar,' said Bill at her side. ' One at Farmers Lane too.'

Mikaela glanced at him momentarily. Farmers Lane - it was the first time he had mentioned the old house that he had lived in so many years ago. Could he really remember back that far?

'Let's go down for a look.' She felt inside the doorway and discovered a light switch. It came on with a twang, and the wooden stairs were illuminated. Looking down she could see that the steps turned at the bottom into a large room. Very carefully she began her descent.

It was rather cold in the cellar, and extraordinarily dusty. Cobwebs were strewn across every corner, and Daddy Long Legs spiders sat along the roof boards. She took each step carefully, finally reaching the lower room.

Glancing around she could see shelves of glass jars, once used, she assumed, for storing stewed fruit and jams. There was a stack of old suitcases sitting in one corner, next to an old butter churn that could have sold for a hundred dollars in the city. A light fitting that must have come from the seventies lay propped against the wall.

'This is an interesting little find,' she said, half to herself.

'Go home now, Lynny.'

She looked up at Bill, who had stopped half-way down the stairs. His face had changed, and he looked nervous.

'What's the matter, Bill?' Seeing Bill nervous made Mikaela feel nervous too.

'Spiders, Lynny. Bill don't like spiders.'

'They wont hurt you, Bill. Not these ones.'

Bill shook his head, and began to inch his way back up to the door.

'Go home now.'

'Wait, I'll come.' She turned to follow him and her eye caught sight of two more objects that were propped in the far corner of the cellar. One was a narrow fishing pole, and the other was a large rifle. She took a second glance at the rifle and shook off a shiver. Guns were a complete unknown to her. She hurried back up the steps, closing the door of the cellar behind her, and followed Bill outside. He still looked nervous, and she could see that his hands were trembling slightly.

'They're gone now, Bill. They're all gone.'

'Bill don't like spiders, snakes and roaches. That what Bill don't like.'

'Okay.' She put her hand on his arm and smiled warmly at him. 'I'll remember that, Bill. I promise. How about I drive you home? It's a long walk back.'

Bill nodded and then the all-encompassing smile was back on his face.

'Bill like cars. Ferrari, Rover, Saab…'

Mikaela chuckled as they walked back through the front gate.

'I don't think you'll find any of those around here. Mikaela only drives an old ute.'

Bill smiled up at her anyway.

'Bill like cars and Lynny too.'

Her heart melted.

Chapter Seven

Mikaela was in the bedroom, tidying a few things before the evening meal. Down the hall in the kitchen the chicken pieces were grilling quietly, releasing a delicious smell that wafted throughout the house. As she put some clothes away, her thoughts turned to Bill and the new friendship she had begun with him. He had chatted to her all the way to Elizabeth's house, and she had been absorbed by his light-hearted nature and simple joy of life. It was as if his soul was not troubled, as if he knew there existed a higher power in charge…

She smiled to herself and turned off the bedside lamp, and the room was immediately plunged into darkness. It never ceased to amaze her how black the night was in the country. For a moment she stood still, getting her bearings, then she moved across to the window to peer out through the curtains. There was no light outside either, only the stars winking at her. No streetlights, no house lights, no cars. Her eyes struggled to make out any shape at all. From the orchard came a slow squeal of metal as the old windmill turned in the breeze. It sounded sad and eerie and she felt a shiver creep down her spine. It was time to get back to the kitchen and the homely sounds of cooking.

*****

'We need some chooks.' Half an hour later Thomas was tucking into the grilled chicken. Even though the pieces were small, they were delicious, and Mikaela decided it was probably quite worthwhile having the fish man arrive with chicken every so often.

'Chooks?' she repeated, chewing a mouthful of vegetables. 'To eat?'

'No, for eggs. I didn't keep chooks here when I was by myself because I didn't need to use many eggs.'

'Do you – do we have a yard or something to keep them in?'

Thomas nodded, wiping his fingers on a paper serviette.

'Dad built a great chook pen, way up behind the orchard. It's still in good nick, and he even invented a water trough that refills automatically. He used a cistern float.'

Mikaela nodded thoughtfully as she ate her meal.

'Thomas, I know nothing about chooks, except how to cook them – and then they have to be pre-packaged. You'll have to teach me how to look after them.'

'There's nothing to chooks, Mikaela. You feed and water them and they lay eggs.'

'How do you know the eggs won't have chickens in them?'

Thomas looked at her sideways, something she had grown accustomed to since her first meeting with him outside the Turramore general store.

'We make sure we don't introduce a rooster.'

'Oh yes, of course. How silly of me…' She giggled for a

moment and Thomas shook his head.

'You're a funny bird, Mikaela girl.'

*****

Helen McDowell picked up Mikaela the following morning and they drove slowly westward in Helen's old white hatchback. The older woman sat in the driver's seat, barely able to see over the top of the steering wheel, her silver hair styled nicely and smelling of lavender and roses.

'I don't take the car out much anymore,' she mentioned casually as they tootled along the road. 'It's good to give it a bit of exercise, and I'm really looking forward to seeing Marg again for a chat.'

Thomas had rung his mother and organised for her to take Mikaela to a farm to the north-west of McDowell Hill, owned by a Mrs Marg Allan. She was a friend of Helen's, and she also sold chickens, so it would make for a nice day out for all concerned. Travelling as slowly as they were right now, Mikaela wondered if they would actually be home in time for tea that evening, but at least it gave her the chance to have a good look at the surrounding country. She had never had a reason to travel west of her new home.

The surrounding farmland was being prepared for sowing, which would start as soon as the rains fell. Tractors here and there were hard at work digging up the dark brown earth, 'working the ground over', in readiness for the seed planting. Thomas was doing the same back on his and Mikaela's property.

After a while a house appeared on the left, a small cottage set a long way back from the road and hardly visible among the large pepper trees and surrounding gums. It was the first residence Mikaela had seen since they had left McDowell Hill.

'Who lives there?' she asked Helen.

73

'Mrs Hamilton. She's a funny cranky old thing – her husband passed away a long time ago, and she just lives there by herself.'

'My closest neighbour…' Mikaela murmured to herself as they passed the house.

They continued west, passing more farms and homesteads, until they came upon an ancient cemetery.

'This is Kenmare,' whispered Helen, in a hush of reverence. An equally ancient stone building followed not long after the cemetery. A council sign at the front of the ruins read 'This is the site of Kenmare Primary School'.

'That school was closed many many years ago.'

'Is that all there is in Kenmare – just a school and a cemetery?'

'That's all there is. No-one lives in this town anymore.'

Mikaela found it a very strange concept, being brought up in the city, to discover an Australian town that had 'died'. No doubt it was a consequence of people moving away from the farming life and its uncertainty, to find employment in the larger towns and cities. As the car drove on through the silent village, she could almost sense a sadness in the atmosphere, as if the whole place grieved over what had been lost.

Helen slowed the car and turned right into a small laneway.

'This is Marg's place up here,' she said, and it wasn't long before they had arrived at the open white gates of a farm. They drove steadily down the dirt driveway, and Mikaela saw the house and further away a long low shed, which she assumed must house the chickens.

A woman came out to greet them as they pulled up in front of the house gate, smiling broadly, her arms flying out in front of her.

'Helen! It's so good to see you!' She gave Helen a mighty embrace, nearly knocking the smaller lady off her feet as she climbed from the car.

'You too, Marg. It's been quite a while since we've have tea and cake together.'

Helen turned to Mikaela.

'Mikaela, this is Marg Allan, a good friend from many years ago. Marg, this is my new daughter-in-law, Mikaela.'

'It's lovely to meet you,' and Marg shook Mikaela's hand strongly. She was tall and sinewy, her face browned by the sun and hard work, her hair cut short in a practical style. She wore long trousers and a neat blouse. 'You've come to get some chickens, haven't you? Come in and have a cup of tea, then I'll send my grandson Hugh out to get them for you.'

The house was large and old, but clean and very tidy, and the cup of tea was lovely after the drive. Mikaela nibbled on a piece of hedgehog slice as she listened to the two women talking and laughing together, watching the light sparkle in their eyes. It occurred to her that here was another woman who was 'alone' in life. She had lost her husband a number of years ago, as had Helen. Somehow the two of them had kept going. Mikaela thought back to the house they had passed which belonged to Mrs Hamilton. She was also alone.

There was a movement at the back door and a boy of about sixteen shuffled into the room, tall, thin and pimply, and smelling of dirt.

'This is my grandson, Hugh. He works here. Hugh, this is Mrs McDowell and Mrs McDowell…' Helen caught Mikaela's eye and smiled at her warmly. Marg continued. 'Mikaela is going to buy some chickens, about five or six, so could you take her down to the shed and pick some out?'

The boy nodded wordlessly and went outside again. Mikaela turned to Helen.

'Did you want to come and help me choose?'

Helen shook her head and took another sip of her tea.

'Oh no, my dear. I hate chickens.'

'You do?'

'She's absolutely petrified of them,' laughed Marg loudly.

'Must have had a bad experience with them when I was little. Can't remember anything, but there you go, I can't stand them all the same.'

'Hugh's good with chickens,' smiled Marg. 'He'll help you choose a few.'

Mikaela got up from her chair, placed the teacup on the table and followed the boy outside.

The sun was bright and the air cool. A slope ran down from the back of the house to the large shed. Taking a longer look, Mikaela could see now that there were dozens of black chickens moving in and out of the shed and pecking at the ground inside the fence line. The term 'free-range' suddenly made sense. She trailed after Hugh, slightly nervous at the prospect of catching the feathery creatures. Did chickens peck in self-defence? Maybe Helen had a good reason for her fear.

As she drew closer, she became aware of a constant cackling noise. At first it was just in the background and then the noise of the birds became louder, an incessant clucking with an occasional squawk. Hugh opened the gate and as they walked in, a huge surge of fussing black feathers and scratching claws came towards them. Mikaela hesitated. She hadn't realised that chickens could be quite large. Some of them seemed to reach her knee, especially when they were fluffed out and squawking.

'They seem a bit…agitated,' she said, eyeing them suspiciously.

'Lookin' for food,' was all that Hugh offered. He reached beside the fence and produced a wooden crate, flinging it in front of them.

'Okay, pick what you want.'

'Oh…um…' Mikaela cast her eye across what seemed like hundreds of black moving hens, at the same time glancing at the crate. One side was made of wire mesh, presumably so that the chickens could breathe once inside. At the end of the box there was a hinged lid that was latched shut. At the other end a square hole had been cut out from the wood. But the whole crate was quite small. He was going to fit six chooks into that?

She looked back over the yard. It was hopeless. There was absolutely no way she could choose one chicken over another – they all looked the same.

'Look, I really have no idea what's a good chook to pick – could you help me?'

Hugh obviously knew chickens back to front. He had sized up two in no time and in one swift movement had them dangling upside down from his fists, flapping and screeching.

'Just tip that box up so I can put 'em in through the hole.'

'Through the hole? Don't you open up the other end?' She tipped the box up so that the small square hole was at the top.

'Nup. They'd flap around too much and get away from yer. Gotta stick 'em through the hole.'

'There is absolutely no way you're going to fit that…'

Before she had time to finish, the lad had pushed the first squawking creature through the hole and into the box. The second was squeezed in a moment later. They cackled and muttered to themselves inside.

Mikaela shook her head in amazement.

'I can't believe that. How did you get them to fit?'

'Mainly feather, not much fat. Pretty easy to squeeze 'em.'

He headed out across the yard and picked out another two birds. When he came back to put them into the crate, he was smiling to himself.

'I just figured out who you are.'

'Mikaela McDowell. Your grandmother already introduced us.'

'I know. But I was yackin' to Joey the other day, and now I've figured out who you are.' There was the smirk again as he stuffed a bird into the crate.

Mikaela took a slow deep breath in and out. Joey Boland, the fish man, had been visiting.

'I don't particularly want to discuss my introduction to Mr Boland.'

'Pretty funny, though.' He pushed the last chicken through the hole. Mikaela looked at the poor feathery huddle compressed in the box.

'I think four might be enough.' It was time to get away.

Hugh caught one more chicken, a scrawny looking thing.

'I'll put this one in, it's pretty small.'

Mikaela looked away as the chicken was shoved into the box with its mates.

'All done.' Hugh wiped his hands on the legs of his dusty jeans then hoisted the crate onto his shoulders, black feathers sticking out from the mesh in all directions. 'Gran thought it was pretty funny too.'

'You told your grandmother? My goodness. And there I was, having a cup of tea with her.'

'I wouldn't worry about Gran,' Hugh chuckled as they walked back up the slope to the house. 'She once went skinny-dippin' in the dam, and the whole fire brigade was sittin' in the next paddock havin' a good ol' laugh.'

'How embarrassing. Poor lady.'

'Nah. She loved it!'

*****

The chickens were loaded into the back of Helen's car, box

and all. Marg asked her guests to stay on for lunch, but Helen declined politely and she and Mikaela eventually made their way home, Helen appearing a little more nervous at the wheel as the sound of quiet clucking floated up from the back of the car.

By the time Helen left Mikaela at McDowell Hill, it was early afternoon and a cold chill was in the air. Mikaela carried the box of poultry up through the wintry bare orchard to the large chicken pen. The pen was made of chicken wire that extended up from all four sides to form a roof as well. Thomas had told her that the pen had a roof to prevent foxes from climbing the sides and getting in through the top. The whole area was large and roomy and high enough to stand in quite easily. A covered section inside the back of the pen had a small kind of ladder leading up to a shelf, and was for the chickens to roost on at night.

Mikaela squatted down in the pen after closing the gate behind her, and carefully opened up the door of the crate. She gave the box a light shake, and one by one the chickens tumbled into the outside world. She watched as the five of them shivered and stumbled around the yard for a while, then began pecking hesitantly at the ground. She smiled at them - they were in a new home, as was she. Four of the chickens were sleek and glossy black, one with a flush of copper across its chest. The fifth was smaller and seemed to have lost some of the feathers from its rear.

'Poor little chook,' Mikaela found herself muttering as she watched it stagger around. 'She looks like a Millicent.'

As she watched them, other names came into her head. One of the chooks looked like a Gabrielle, another one was Eugenie, and still another was Gertrude. The big one with the copper flush had to be Henrietta.

'I've named you,' Mikaela found herself talking to the birds. 'How many farmers name their chooks? What's wrong with me? Now I'm talking to you…'

She went back outside to get a jug of pellets from a large bag sitting in the shed beside the chicken pen.

'Here's some food, chookies.' She tipped the pellets onto the ground and watched the birds scramble around her feet, then she swished out the water trough with an old broom and waited until it re-filled. While she waited she let her eyes wander from the chicken yard to the orchard, where most of the trees had lost their leaves, the foliage now lying in soggy piles on the ground. She looked further away to the house, sitting still and silent, its burgundy and green trimmings looking pale in the afternoon light, quietly waiting for her. The isolation of the countryside began to seep into her consciousness again. Maybe she could stay here with the chickens until Thomas came home – at least they were company.

A squawk from one of her new friends brought her back to reality. She stood the broom up against the wire and quietly closed the gate behind her, heading back towards the house.

Thomas was late home that evening. Mikaela went to bed and fell asleep, leaving his tea in the fridge.

Chapter Eight

The following morning as Mikaela scooped out a jug of chicken pellets, she heard the sound of a plane.

The sky was beginning to cloud over and she was wondering if she should bring in her washing. Thomas had left early in the morning to work on the tractor, so the laundry had kept her mind off of her isolation. Methodically sorting the clothes and hanging them out to dry had given her something to concentrate on, a task to perform that provided meaning to the day. It was strange that such a mundane activity had become so important for her survival...

Looking up now, she saw the small red and white striped aircraft flying westward, past the farm, following the road. She stood with the jug in her hand, her eyes fixed on the plane, her heart giving a strange thump. It was the same one she had seen flying over the town when she had lived in the teacher house. She watched it until it disappeared, then sighed loudly, the breath shuddering through her body. She had certainly felt safer in town. There were people who lived next door, there were shops and a railway station – there was community. Out here at McDowell Hill, there was only loneliness.

She caught herself in her thoughts. Was that really how she felt – lonely? She had a wonderful husband, a gorgeous house, and friends just out of town. She even had some chickens. Why on earth would she feel lonely?

She fingered the jug in her hand then slowly ran her hands across the rusty chicken wire of the pen beside her. Yes, it was loneliness, she decided – loneliness born of unfamiliarity. She had a yard here for the chickens, but she didn't know how it had been made or the man who had made it. She had a house, but it had been built in another era, for another family. Unknown hands had planted the orchard years ago – what if she did the wrong thing and the trees died? She was an outsider, unfamiliar with the deeper meaning of the land and its ways.

And everyone else was very familiar with everything. They had been born here in the country and had grown up in its bosom, close to its beating heart. Thomas had worked long hours coaxing the land into giving him its best crops. David did the same on his property and Emily nursed those wounded by it harshness. Helen was involved with its community, and understood the importance of cropping, harvest and the men folk working long into the night. She understood the soul of the country. Everybody did – everybody except Mikaela. And Mikaela felt alone.

She found herself sighing again as she replaced the jug and closed up the shed door. The sky was looking more ominous by the minute and the air was chilly. This would be the big rain that would signal the beginning of cropping. Thomas had been so busy lately that she had hardly seen him. Once cropping started she wouldn't see him at all.

By dinnertime, the first drops had begun. The temperature

had fallen significantly and the day had grown dark. Mikaela had to light the Coonara to warm the house and switch on the kitchen fluorescent to prepare a tuna pie for dinner. She heard the tap running in the laundry outside and then Thomas was pulling off his boots as he came in through the kitchen door. He shook the drops of water from his hair and brushed down his sweatshirt with his hands.

'Cold and wet out there,' he muttered, then he came behind Mikaela and gave her a squeeze. 'How's your morning been?'

'Fine,' she answered, kissing his moist cheek and smelling grease on his clothes. 'Hung out the washing, fed the chooks…missed you…'

'I missed you too,' and he kissed the top of her head then let her go to move over to the table. 'This is a crazy time of year, getting ready for cropping. And now that it's raining, we'll be starting tomorrow hopefully, as long as the ground isn't boggy. I've almost finished getting the air seeder ready.'

'You have to go back out again after lunch?'

'Yep. Won't be too long I hope.' He helped himself to the pie.

'Can I come with you?' Mikaela asked, wiping her hands on the towel by the sink. 'To help?'

'Nah, I'll be right. It's pretty dirty work, all grease and muck. You'd do better to keep inside and stay warm.'

It felt as if a heavy stone had been dropped into her chest.

Thomas washed down the pie with a glass of juice, then got up to switch on the kettle.

'I'll make us a cuppa,' he said, then he glanced at Mikaela as she sat slowly down at the table. 'Are you alright, Mrs McDowell?'

Mikaela nodded and tried to form her lips into a smile.

'I guess so. I'm just a bit…lonely, I think.'

Thomas let the kettle boil, then made two cups of tea and

brought them to the table. He stirred sugar into his cup, and when he spoke his voice was gentle.

'It's not hard to get lonely out here. Especially when you've just arrived. I used to get lonely too.'

'What did you do about it?' Mikaela felt her voice crack and hoped she wouldn't cry. Thomas looked up at her for a moment, but she managed to control her emotions.

'I'd get out and go to town, visit Mum or Andy or David. Sometimes I'd just sit by the fire and think about Dad. Dad would never get lonely or down. He was an inspiration.'

'I'm sure it's just a phase,' Mikaela murmured. 'I don't want you to think I'm an idiot.'

'I would never think that.' He got up and leaned over the table to kiss her gently on the lips. 'And remember, I always want you tell me things. Never be afraid to tell me how you feel.'

She nodded, desperately wanting to fall apart in his arms. But he had work to do, and she didn't want him to see her weaknesses. She finally managed the smile, and he returned it then rose to take his plates to the sink.

'I'd better keep going, Mikaela girl. I'm not far away if you need me.'

He left her with the screen door banging behind him. A moment later, his head popped back in.

You have a visitor,' he smiled and left again as through the door came Bill.

'Hello Lynny,' he grinned.

Mikaela jumped up to take his wet umbrella and help him off with his muddy shoes.

'Bill, did you walk from Elizabeth's house again? In the rain?'

'Yep.'

'Come and sit in front of the fire where you can warm up.' She took him into the living room where the fire was crackling in the corner and he sat on the lounge suite, his jumper smelling of wet wool. Mikaela went back into the kitchen and served out some pie and a glass of water.

'Here, have something to eat,' and she gave it to Bill who gratefully wolfed the food down. 'I can't believe you walked all that way again.'

'Like to walk.'

'Yes, but your heart…'

'Don't matter. Like to walk.'

'I must talk to Elizabeth about this…' Mikaela murmured to herself.

After a while, Bill put his empty plate on the coffee table and then held his hands out to the blaze behind the glass.

'Nice fire,' he said. Mikaela sat across from him and stretched her feet towards the warmth.

'It is a nice fire, Bill.'

'Like the copper house fire. Nice and warm.'

'The what?'

'Warm in the copper house.' He was silent for a moment, and then he looked over at Mikaela, a struggle playing out across his face. The firelight glowed on his skin. 'Bill put it in the copper house.'

There was an intensity coming from his eyes, burning into her own, which made her catch her breath.

'What, Bill? What did you put in the copper house?'

'Yours, Lynny. You give it to Bill.'

'Lynny gave you something?'

'Bill hide it for you.'

Mikaela went to her knees in front of her uncle and took his hands.

'Oh Bill, I'm not Lynny. I'm Mikaela. I'm Lynny's… daughter.' She searched his face for understanding but he turned back to the fire, his eyes lost in the flames.

'Nice and warm in the copper house,' he muttered.

The room was silent for a long time. Mikaela let go of Bill's hands but remained on the floor, soaking up the warmth of the fire and watching the flames lick over the Mallee root. Bill's words floated inside her head, but there was so much information missing. Bill sat contentedly on the lounge suite.

'Do you ever get lonely, Bill?' Mikaela finally asked, her mind going back to her thoughts of the morning.

'Lonely? Not Bill. Bill got Jesus.'

Mikaela's mouth fell open.

'Jesus?'

'Jesus here. Bill not lonely.'

'How do know about Jesus, Bill?'

'You tell me, Lynny.'

'I did? I mean...' She shook her head. At one point Carolyn must have told Bill about Jesus.

'What else did Lynny tell you, Bill?'

'Just Jesus. And use a hanky!' He laughed and clapped his hands. 'Use a hanky and not forget to zip up!' He mimed zipping us his trousers, and chuckled uncontrollably. Mikaela couldn't help laughing as well.

'You are a funny fellow, Bill.'

'Yep, funny fellow Bill.' They smiled at each other, then Bill patted Mikaela's head.

'Lynny not lonely now. Jesus here.'

'I know, Bill,' Mikaela whispered. 'He is here. Sometimes I forget.'

The rain outside suddenly intensified, making a drumming sound on the roof. Mikaela glanced out the window.

'You won't be able to walk home today Bill. I'll drive you. Would you like to go in the ute again?'

Bill nodded enthusiastically, and they went back to the kitchen to retrieve his shoes and umbrella. Mikaela decided to have a chat with Elizabeth about Bill's walking exploits. She worried about his health.

The driveway outside was slowly turning into a quagmire but the smell of rain on the dirt was wonderful. They quickly bundled themselves into the ute, the rain heavy on the roof, and Mikaela started the engine and headed up the driveway. She was about to turn east towards town when she hesitated, leaving the engine idling at the roadside.

'Bill, would you like to visit my nearest neighbour?'

Bill nodded and without a second thought, Mikaela turned to head west. Thomas had told her earlier that it was a good idea to get out of the house and socialise. She had a spare hour and as far as she knew Bill didn't have to be back at Elizabeth's at a specified time. It was a great opportunity to drop in on Mrs Hamilton.

She followed the road west, keeping her eye out for the little house that she had seen set back among the trees. The ute's windscreen wipers struggled to keep the rain off the glass, so they travelled slowly. Eventually they came to a mailbox tin and turned left into the long driveway.

The house was very small when it finally came into view, similar to McDowell Hill in style but a fraction of the size. It was a dirty white colour and had paint peeling from its walls. Mikaela pulled the ute up alongside an old picket fence at the front of the house, its palings missing in many places. She got out quickly, with Bill following, and together they pushed open a squeaky little gate and ran up the pathway through the rain to the shelter of the verandah. Here beside the front door was an old armchair, it's paisley fabric tattered and worn. A few old buckets lay on the rotting wooden boards of the verandah and further along sat an old cream can. Dirt and dust were everywhere, and with the grey sky and constant rain, the whole house appeared rather dismal.

As Mikaela stood at the front door, she suddenly felt nervous at the prospect of meeting the old lady. Helen had said she was cranky. It has been a challenge getting to know Gareth and his cranky ways, but she wasn't sure if she could do it all over again with Mrs Hamilton.

She jangled the rusty bell that was hanging beside the door. There was movement from inside, and after a moment the door was opened by a bony old woman with grey mussed up hair and a faded floral apron across her front. She had a long thin nose and tightly pressed lips and a grey cardigan hung over her sloping shoulders.

'Yes, what do you want?' The voice was nasal and whiny.

'Hello, I'm Mikaela McDowell. I just wanted to drop in and say thank-you for lighting the fire at our house the night we came back from our honeymoon.'

The woman grunted and her eyes slid to Bill.

'Who's yer friend?'

'This is my uncle, William Farmer.'

There was a moment's silence, and the woman looked as if she might make a derogatory comment. She must have thought better of it, to Mikaela's relief, and instead introduced herself.

'I'm Bonnie Hamilton. You can come in if yer like.' She opened the door wider and the visitors stepped inside.

The musty dank smell hit them immediately and was almost overpowering. Old wallpaper hung in sad strips from the walls in the small living room and the curtains appeared dark and mouldy. A vase of dead flowers stood on a chair.

'Come through to the kitchen and I'll put the kettle on.'

The thought of a mouldy cup wasn't pleasant.

'Please don't go to any trouble, Mrs Hamilton.'

'No trouble. My nephew arrived this morning and he'll be wanting a cuppa too, no doubt.'

They walked into the dingy kitchen where an old brown laminate table was surrounded by four brown vinyl chairs, all in need of repair. A young man rose from one of these chairs, where he had been reading a newspaper.

'Zachary, this is Mikaela and William, from McDowell Hill.'

'It's nice to meet you,' said the man, shaking Mikaela's hand. His brown eyes smiled at her from under a boyish lock of dark hair, and his skin was tanned and unblemished. 'Call me Zac.'

Mikaela smiled back, aware of the touch of his hand in hers. Then in a scene that felt like it was being played out in slow motion, she let go of his hand, and turning to face Mrs Hamilton, caught sight of something red and white through the kitchen window.

In the drizzle of rain outside sat the plane.

Chapter Nine

'Would yer like more sugar?'

Mikaela shook her head and politely declined, pushing nervously at the cup on her lap. Bonnie Hamilton passed a plate of biscuits to Bill, who happily took two and sat munching contentedly. From across the living room in his chair, Zac watched the scene silently, a slight smile on his lips, his narrow dark fingers playing at the threads from the worn upholstery.

'Haven't had a proper visitor for years,' Mrs Hamilton was saying, 'You shoulda rang first and I woulda had somethin' baked. Woulda cleaned up a bit.'

'I didn't want you to go to any trouble,' Mikaela murmured.

She heard Zac clear his throat.

'So you married into the McDowell clan? Thomas, right?'

'Yes, do you know him?'

Zac nodded.

'I believe we went to high school together. He was a few years ahead of me.'

'That's nice.' Mikaela took a sip of her tea, tasting grit on her tongue, and glanced at Bill who was onto his fourth biscuit.

'I remember his father,' piped in Mrs Hamilton. 'He was a fine strapping man. Pity he went so early. Like Cecil.'

'Cecil?'

'Cecil was my husband. And his younger brother Frederick was Zachary's father.' She poured herself more tea. 'Poor dear, that one. Brain wasn't screwed on right. Would you like another cup?'

'No thank you,' Mikaela replied, aware of Zac bristling slightly.

'You don't need to speak of my father like that, Aunty,' he said softly, training his dark eyes on her face.

'Well, he was a bit odd, Zac. He used to be real excited about somethin', some new thing he was inventin' in the old shed, then the next day he'd be all sour about it. Change like the wind, he would - Cecil could never figure him out.' She stirred her tea. 'Then he used to beat you and your poor mother, didn't he? Probably just as well he got knocked down by that train.'

A silence fell over the living room. All that Mikaela could hear was Bill at her side, licking crumbs from his lips. Across from her, Zac's face had turned pale, and she looked away from him quickly. How could his aunt have just blurted out all that private information to two strangers? All at once she felt a strange sorrow for the pilot.

'Could we see your plane, Zac?' she asked, determined to end the current topic of conversation.

Zac appeared to take control of himself and flashed her a dazzling smile. The fringe of dark hair fell across his eyes as he got up from his chair.

'Sure.'

They went outside through the back door. The rain had abated for a moment and the sun was making a feeble attempt to poke through the clouds. The air was fresh and cold. Mikaela was aware of Mrs Hamilton watching them from the kitchen window.

The backyard of the house was in a similar state to the front. There were old tins scattered about, a rusted wheelbarrow lying upside down, and some timber propped up against a wall. Over to the right, Mikaela saw a chicken yard not unlike the one at McDowell Hill. A number of scrawny black hens were pecking at the ground.

The plane was tied down not far from the house. It had a single propeller at its nose, and a broad red stripe down each side. They walked slowly over to the aircraft and Mikaela put a finger out to touch the edge of a wing, wondering to herself how something so light and flimsy could make it into the air.

'It's a Piper Pawnee,' Zac was saying, seemingly recovered from his aunt's slanderous comments. 'Foxtrot Juliet Echo.'

'Sorry?'

'That's the call sign, its registration. FJE. Foxtrot Juliet Echo is what you say over the radio, to make it sound clearer.'

'And you use this plane to spray the crops?'

'That's right. It's got a big cavity in the nose here, almost big enough to fit a person in actually. That's where the spray goes.'

'Don't you get scared up there, so high?'

'No, I love it.' His face had a wistful look and he stroked the wing of the plane. 'I can get away from it all, leave it all behind. Do you ever get a chance to do that?'

'Well, not in a plane…'

'I'll take you flying one day. Not in the Pawnee, because there's only one seat. But I could borrow the Mooney from my boss.'

'Um, maybe not. I think I'd be too scared.' She smiled nervously and he laughed.

'There's nothing to be scared of…' he said softly, holding her gaze. The air prickled between them, and she moved away suddenly, bumping into Bill.

'What do you think, Bill?' she asked brightly. 'Do you like planes?'

Her uncle beamed.

'Bill like planes a lot, Lynny.'

'Maybe you can come too one day,' said Zac.

'That would be like Granny Green's knees!'

Zac raised his eyebrows and Mikaela put her arm through Bill's.

'That means it would be great,' she explained with a smile. 'I think.' She glanced at her watch.

'We really should get going. I need to take Bill back to his sister's place.'

'That would be Elizabeth Scott?'

Mikaela was taken aback.

'Yes, how did you know?'

Zac smiled and looked away, dropping his head as if shy.

'I'm pretty good at information gathering. I know all the farms around here, who lives where, the shape of the land from the sky, how many dams each farmer has. And I know your house too.' The dark eyes were looking into hers once more, making her feel strangely uncomfortable.

'You do?'

'Yes. The night of your tin kettling – I lit the fire.'

*****

As the ute bumped up the Henty Highway, Mikaela took a

deep breath and reflected on the day's events. What a strange pair were Bonnie Hamilton and her nephew. Mrs Hamilton had explained before they left that Zac landed his plane in the paddock behind her house whenever he was doing work around the Turramore area, and then he would stay on for a night or two. Mikaela wondered whether they had an amicable relationship. If Bonnie was always bringing up the past as she had done today, surely Zac would not find it easy to stay at her house for very long. Maybe he felt an obligation to check on her, being alone and isolated as she was. Then again, maybe it was part of Zac's whole 'escape' idea, to get away for a while onto an isolated farm, although Mikaela didn't think escape could come very easily in the company of his aunt.

She turned the ute through the gates of the Scott property and Elizabeth met them at the back door of the house.

'I tried ringing you, but there was no-one home,' she said, giving them both a hug. Her voice sounded strained. 'I was hoping William had found his way to McDowell Hill again.'

They entered the house together and Mikaela and her uncle warmed up for a moment in front of the heater.

'William, honey, why don't you go and have a lie down? You've had a busy day.' Elizabeth gave her brother a worried smile and he nodded.

'Yep, Bill sleep now.'

Mikaela watched him trundle out of the room, then turned to her aunt who was pouring out tea.

'I'm not sure Bill should be doing so much walking around,' she said, taking the cup that was offered to her. 'I mean, is he all that well?'

Elizabeth settled into an easy chair beside Mikaela, and fiddled with the cup and saucer in her hands, her brow creased.

'I know what you're saying, Mikaela. I'm not sure what to do. I had to drop some things in to the school today, and I left William here going through some old books we'd found. By the time I'd got back, he was gone. He just loves walking, it's all he knows back in Sydney. And he's got an amazing sense of direction.'

Mikaela nodded.

'Okay, but you haven't answered my question. Is he well, Elizabeth?'

Her aunt tilted her head in a worried way, the creases intensifying on her forehead. It was a look Mikaela was beginning to recognise. It meant there was more behind the story.

'When I first made arrangements for William to come and stay,' she began, 'his overseers told me his heart condition had worsened. He's always had heart problems, ever since he was born.'

'That's part of the syndrome?'

'It can be, apparently. Then there's his blood. It's not that good at fighting off infection. Something about his white blood cells…?'

Mikaela nodded, vague memories of her studies at university coming back to her.

'You know, Mikaela, he's getting old too, for a person with his condition.'

'I had wondered about that.'

They sat in silence for a while, sipping their drinks, then Elizabeth sighed.

'I really don't think we can stop him walking,' she said finally. 'He loves it so much. It would be a shame to take that away from him.'

'I suppose it gives him some control over his life,' Mikaela commented. She smiled as she thought of Bill. 'He's so easy going, Elizabeth. Nothing seems to worry him. Except spiders, that is.'

'Yes, I know what you mean. He's very easy to live with. He'll be returning to Sydney soon - I'm going to miss him.'

Mikaela nodded pensively. I'll miss him too, she thought. And then the loneliness will overtake me.

*****

Thomas arrived home late that night, looking worn out from driving the tractor over the paddocks and planting the wheat that would hopefully yield a bumper crop at Christmas time. Mikaela sat at the kitchen table in her dressing gown, a hot Milo in her hand, while Thomas ate his meal in silence. She could tell he was exhausted, the lines on his face deeper than normal, his broad shoulders hunched slightly over his plate. But she longed to tell him of her day.

'I visited Mrs Hamilton this morning.'

Thomas took a moment to respond, then nodded as he put a forkful of mashed potato into his mouth.

'Bonnie Hamilton,' he said through the potato. 'Haven't seen her for a long time.'

'She had her nephew with her. Zac Hamilton. He flies that plane we were talking about.'

Thomas was still chewing so she continued.

'He seemed a nice sort of guy. He said he went to high school with you.'

'Zac Hamilton…' he repeated, 'I remember the name. I didn't realise he was the bloke flying for the region now.'

'Apparently his father was a bit…odd. Do you remember a Frederick Hamilton?'

This time Thomas put his fork down on his plate, and squinted up at the opposite wall, frowning in weary concentration.

'I do actually. He did himself in – stepped in front of a train.'

'He killed himself?'

'I remember when it happened. I was in year eleven. But I don't remember Zac all that well – he must have been younger than me.'

He went back to his meal, falling into the silence that seemed to be so much a part of their conversation at this busy time of the year. Mikaela slowly twirled her mug, watching the milky liquid lap at the sides, and thought again about the events of the day. Frederick Hamilton must have been a very distressed man to have taken his own life and leave his son behind. And yet Bonnie had said he had been 'knocked down' by a train, as if it was an accident. Perhaps the community had accepted the fact it had been a suicide but the family was still in denial.

Either way, it was a tragedy, and she told herself she would not bring the subject up at all next time she saw Zac. She caught herself in her thoughts. There wouldn't be a 'next time', not unless she dropped in to Bonnie's house again when he was there, and there would be no reason for her to do that…

Thomas had finished eating and got up to shuffle through the kitchen towards the hallway.

'I'm going to have a shower and hit the sack,' he said, squeezing his fingers over his tired eyes. 'It's going to be a big day tomorrow.' He managed a smile in her direction, his blue eyes weary, and then he was gone.

Mikaela finished her Milo, the last mouthful tasting lukewarm and gravelly.

Chapter Ten

On Sunday, Mikaela sat alone at church. Thomas had stayed home on the farm to continue cropping before the next rains came to soak in the seeds, something he didn't like to do on a Sunday but the weather was the dictator of life in the Mallee. David was home doing the same, and Emily had been called in to work at Leighton. Helen was at home with a cold, and there was no sign of Andy, who was probably at David's helping in whatever way possible. It was such a strange time of the year. Cropping only took a few weeks, but they were the longest weeks Mikaela could ever remember.

As she listened to the minister's words, she felt a struggle beginning to disturb her heart. She had sat here in the church many times before and had felt at peace. Today a niggling doubt crept into her mind. Perhaps she was not really suited to the country after all. Maybe she had rushed into her marriage with Thomas without considering all the facts. She had certainly not realised beforehand how often she would be forced to go about daily life without him. Suddenly the years as a farmer's wife stretched before her intolerably and eternally...

The final hymn had started, but as Mikaela stood, the desire to sing left her, and she put down her hymnbook and walked quickly out of the church.

*****

The following morning, Mikaela returned to Turramore Primary to continue teaching. She had been looking forward to getting back into a routine ever since she and Thomas had returned from their honeymoon. She readied herself early, organised her books and left the house at the same time as Thomas. They kissed quickly, and she watched him walk down to the sheds as she got into her ute. She thought that going back to work would make it easier to say good-bye, but it didn't. In fact, leaving Thomas on the farm while she worked in town all day was just another strange feeling altogether.

Gareth was already in his classroom when she arrived, a mug of coffee steaming beside him. The mornings had become decidedly chilly, and the heaters had been turned on in both classrooms.

He greeted her now with a wide smile.

'Turramore's favourite teacher is back. It's good to see you, Mikaela.' They embraced, and Mikaela pulled up a chair beside her father.

'Did you miss me?'

'Absolutely. Not just me – your whole class missed you.'

Mikaela grinned.

'I am really looking forward to seeing them all again. It's so good to be back...' She hesitated, trying to identify her feelings.

'How's Thomas?'

'Busy. Very busy.'

'Cropping has come at an unfortunate time for you two. Never mind, it doesn't last forever.'

Mikaela tried to smile.

'Doesn't it? It feels like it does. Then there's harvest time, and that takes even longer.'

Gareth looked at her sharply.

'Do I detect a hint of melancholy in your voice?'

Mikaela shrugged.

'I guess I'm just a bit down at the moment. We had such a lovely time in Tasmania, and now I've hit reality with a thud.'

'That happens, Mikaela,' Gareth said, surprisingly gently. 'Not just in a marriage relationship, but with any 'honeymoon' period – starting a new job, moving to a new place. You'll get used to life here again.'

'I know. I'm being silly. Maybe it's just hormonal.'

'I'm not going there,' Gareth chuckled. 'Now, have you got yourself ready for this morning's lessons or do you need some breathing space?'

'I'm fine. Thanks, Gareth.' She placed a kiss on his grey head as she got up to leave. 'I'll see you at assembly.'

The rest of the day went by in a whirl. The children were so happy to see her that Mikaela wasn't sure how much learning actually went on at all. Each child had stories to tell her of their escapades over the last few weeks, and she let them tell, enjoying their enthusiasm and spirit.

The twins especially made her laugh with their conversation.

'Miss Gord – I mean, Mrs McDowell,' Sarah began, 'On Saturday we went…'

'…to the museum at…' said Rebekah.

'…Hillsford, and we saw…'

'…a steam train that…', and so it went on.

By the afternoon, Mikaela was back into the swing of her teaching role, and as she packed her books into the ute at the end of the day she felt a sense of achievement. She had enjoyed the time she had spent at the school and had managed to keep her mind off of her other concerns. Now she climbed into the driver's seat and sat for a moment, leaning her elbows on the wide black steering wheel and taking a deep breath. Yes, she had managed to forget about her loneliness, but now her thoughts turned back to home. She wondered how Thomas was, what he had been doing all day, whether he had missed her, what he had made himself for dinner…

She had missed Thomas all day, without realising it. She had missed Thomas ever since he had left the house that first morning they had woken up together at McDowell Hill. They hadn't really spoken properly since returning to Turramore, and she hoped desperately that this wasn't a taste of the years to come.

She started up the ute and drove out of the school grounds and through the town, turning out onto the west road. The sky before her was magical, the setting sun streaking fairy floss pink across the sky. It did not take long for the McDowell homestead to come into view on the right – she was becoming accustomed to the distances now, and what once had seemed like miles and miles away, was gradually becoming closer.

Turning in to the dirt driveway, she brought the ute around the peppertree and parked alongside the front fence. The air was cooling off considerably, and she gathered her books and hurried through the front gate with thoughts of getting the Coonara going once she was inside. Coming around the corner of the house and heading towards the back door, she suddenly stopped with a jerk, a strong uncanny feeling of eyes upon her. Looking up, she saw a man with rakish hair across his face leaning casually against the wall of the laundry block, hands in his jeans pockets, smart navy shirt over his slim form. He stood upright as she came forward.

'I've caught you at a bad time – I apologise.'

'That's alright, Zac. I've been caught at worse times…' She smiled uncertainly and shifted the books in her arm. 'What can I do for you? Would you like to come in for a cup of tea?'

'Only if you have time.'

She opened the door and he followed, taking a seat at the kitchen table. She put her books down on the bench and went to fill the kettle.

'I was out and about,' he continued, 'and I just thought I'd see if you were home.'

'I'm working again now,' Mikaela explained, setting out the cups. 'I won't be getting home till this time most days. Thomas shouldn't be too much longer either – he usually has afternoon tea before going back out on the tractor.'

'Thomas. I look forward to meeting him again.'

Mikaela poured the tea and sat opposite Zac. She watched him slowly stir in the sugar, looking at the spoon as he did, and wondered if she should break the uncomfortable silence that had descended over the table. Eventually he spoke.

'I just wanted to apologise for my aunty the other day. She tends to exaggerate things a little, and people get a bit turned off by her conversation. I'm sure you didn't need to hear all that.'

Mikaela sipped her tea and composed her thoughts. She wanted to ask Zac how much of what his aunt had said was true, but she knew it was not the right time, nor was it any of her business.

'I was a little embarrassed for your sake,' she offered finally, 'but I'm sure your aunt didn't mean to upset you. That's probably just her way of saying things.'

'Hmm,' murmured Zac, 'I'm not entirely convinced.

Aunty said my dad was 'odd'. I think she's just as bad, if not worse.'

'Does she socialise very much?'

'Hardly ever. That's why I drop in to see her whenever I can, just to give her someone to talk to other than the chooks and the cat.'

'Funny,' Mikaela said thoughtfully, 'I found myself talking to the chooks the other day, and I haven't lived out here half as long as your aunt.'

'You'd better watch yourself then,' laughed Zac.

They sat in silence again for a moment longer.

'How is Thomas going with the cropping?' Zac asked finally.

'Fine, almost finished I think – I hope. I don't see him very much.' As soon as the words left her lips she wished she hadn't said them – they exposed too much of herself and her thoughts. Zac fortunately did not follow up on the comment.

'I was thinking about Thomas the other day, and I'm pretty sure I remember him from school. He's a good footballer, right?'

Mikaela nodded and Zac continued.

'Yes, I remember him helping to coach us little guys. I must have just started high school, and he must have been in the senior year. I remember watching him play – we all thought he was a hero.'

Mikaela smiled at the thought of her husband being a heroic athlete in young eyes.

'I'll have to tell him that. He's probably not even aware of it.'

'Probably not. He's a pretty humble bloke, right? He wouldn't know any of that stuff. I'd love to tell him myself.' There was a brightness around Zac's face as he spoke and a light was gleaming in his dark eyes.

'Stay a bit longer and you might get to,' smiled Mikaela, enjoying the praise that her husband was receiving.

'I'd better not overstay my welcome – thanks for the cuppa anyway.'

'It's a pleasure. Drop in whenever you like.' Again the words of politeness had been spoken before Mikaela had time to think. She hesitated, but there was no way she could drag them back.

'I'm not sure Thomas would appreciate a strange man dropping in to see his new wife,' Zac laughed as he got up from his seat. 'There is a very active grapevine in the country – and I'm not talking about the one across your front verandah.'

'Actually, I know quite a bit about that grapevine,' Mikaela commented as she gathered the teacups. There was a noise from outside and she heard the sound of a tap running.

'That will be Thomas now, washing up for afternoon tea,' she said casually. She noticed Zac straighten and take a breath, his eyes aglow. In the next moment, Thomas was through the door and into the kitchen, looking slightly startled to see the visitor.

'Thomas, this is Zac Hamilton. I was telling you about him the other day.'

'Right, the pilot.' He extended his hand. 'Good to meet you. Can't be doing much flying in this weather.'

Zac shook Thomas' hand with vigour, his arm muscles tight, his breathing slightly ragged. Mikaela could not believe how much the younger man was in awe of the older, and she shook her head, smiling at them.

'No, I've had to stay longer with my aunt, with the clouds socked in like this. Hopefully in the next day or two I'll be able to take off.'

Thomas let go of his hand and pulled back a seat.

'Have you had a drink?'

'Yes, Thomas. Your wife very kindly made me a cup of tea. I was just telling her about high school, how you used to help coach us in football. You were terrific – do you remember?'

Thomas smiled as he sat, but looked confused.

'Perhaps…my memories of high school aren't that great, sorry Zac. But if you remember me doing a good job, then that's the main thing.'

Zac smiled at him, then seemed lost for words. Mikaela decided to help him out.

'You didn't walk all the way from your aunt's, did you Zac? Bill walks all over the place. I don't know how he does it.'

Zac shook his head.

'No, I parked my ute up on the sandy lane behind your property. It just happened to be in the direction I was going when I was surveying the area.'

'So you'll be doing the crop spraying in a few weeks?' Thomas asked.

'Yes, this is my region. I'll be up there in the Pawnee.' He stopped for a moment and glanced at the clock on the wall. 'I'd better go, actually. I should finish up a few things before it gets dark. It's been good to meet you again, Thomas, and thanks for the tea, Mikaela.'

He ran his hand across his dark fringe and waved briefly to them as he went out the kitchen door.

Mikaela watched him leave then lent over to Thomas and kissed him gently.

'Sorry that I had company when you got home – have you had a good day?'

'Busy,' replied Thomas, 'and it's not over yet. That patch on the north-eastern corner is a bit boggy. I'll have to try to get on to it tomorrow.'

'I missed you all day…' breathed Mikaela, running her

hand down his strong neck. 'Will you be late home to-night?'

Thomas nodded, finishing his tea. He must have noticed the sadness in her face, because he smiled and took her hand.

'I'm sorry, hon'. Just a few more days and I will have nailed it. Then we can relax.'

'Until when? Until it starts up all over again?'

'That's just how farming goes. Our work is governed by the weather. We crop after the rain, we harvest before it gets too wet...and we do everything else in between times.' He stroked a rough finger across her cheek. 'You'll get used to it.'

'Maybe.' She pulled away from him, gathering the cups from the table and placing them on the sink. 'I guess I'll leave your tea in the microwave then.'

'Maybe that would be the best.' She heard him get up from his chair and knew that he was standing behind her. She felt his hand softly rest upon her shoulder, but she didn't turn. After a moment the hand was gone, and she heard him pick up his cap and leave through the back door.

She leaned heavily against the sink. I'm such a fool, she thought to herself, closing her eyes and squeezing out the tears. I'm so self-centred. What sort of a wife gets annoyed when her husband is doing all he can to keep bread on the table – literally? But at the same time a voice inside her head reminded her of how it used to be, the time they'd spent together, the hours spent talking, the romance...how could things have changed so much?

She took a deep breath and tried to pull herself together. Life had to go on, no matter what strange confusion was whirling in her mind. She gathered her handbag from the bench and wandered up the hallway to the main bedroom, breathing deeply as she walked. Once there she quietly changed into tracksuit pants and a sweater, then ran the brush through her hair, wiping away the stray tears that remained at the corners of her eyes. As she replaced the brush, her eyes strayed to the drawer where she kept Carolyn's diary. She opened it and pulled out the worn book, taking it with her back out to the living room.

It wasn't long before she had a good blaze going in the Coonara - Mallee roots were excellent for long-burning fires. She sat on the couch, curling her socked feet up under her, and flicked open the diary.

She still had no system of reading the book. She skimmed through the pages until a word leapt out at her, and then she read that entry. To read it from cover to cover felt too much like prying. This way, it was more like she had come upon the diary by accident and was just having a look. Somehow it felt better.

Now as she sat in front of the fire, she was reminded of Bill, warming his hands up in the lounge room and telling her stories about Carolyn. He had mentioned something about a house – a house made of copper. She browsed through the diary, turning the pages gently. She smiled as she read an entry about chickens.

April 3rd, '73
Thought Mary and Kate were off the lay, but found two eggs today. Haven't seen any foxes of late, so perhaps that was the reason they were touchy.

Mikaela chuckled to herself. So she wasn't the only one who named her hens. She skimmed further through the pages and the thoughts of Carolyn Farmer. Finally she came across an entry in the middle of the book.

July 15th, '74
Lost Billy again today. I love him coming to visit, but he wor-
ries me so. He went walking and didn't come back. I pan-
icked at first, then I remembered the copper house, and there
he was. His memories of that place must still be strong. He
was sitting in the corner with his arms out towards the 'fire',
but of course there is no fire there now.

The entry finished, with no further mention of the copper
house. Mikaela closed the book thoughtfully. Next time she
saw Bill, she would ask him about it. He would be leaving
Turramore soon, and she was running out of time.

Chapter Eleven

The remainder of the school week was hectic, dotted with numerous incidents that Mikaela had not encountered before, making her wonder at times why she had been so keen to start working again.

To begin with, three of the children in her class came down with a vomiting illness all on the same day, and none of them were particularly good with bucket usage. The disinfected classroom smelt like a hospital ward.

Another day, a student from Gareth's class tripped over in the playground and smashed his front teeth against the steel pole that was supporting the slippery slide. There was blood all over his face and shirt by the time he was bundled into the first aid room and his parents were contacted. Unfortunately the broken teeth were part of his adult set, and some major dental work would be required in the future.

On the last day of the week, Mikaela walked around the back of the sports equipment shed while on playground duty to find three grade six boys smoking in a dug out hollow.

They saw her at the last minute and quickly stamped out the butts, waving frantically at the air to disperse the wisps of smoke. Then all three stood looking at her, their clothes dishevelled and dirty, but their eyes hard.

Mikaela put her hands on her hips, completely lost for words. She had known these boys for over a year, and they had never been a cause for concern in the past. Disappointment sank deeply into her heart.

'What do you think you're doing?' she finally asked, her voice sounding harsh and thin in her ears.

'Nothin', Mrs McDowell,' said one boy, raising his chin slightly in defiance.

'Don't tell me rubbish, Alex. I saw you. Who said you could bring cigarettes into the school grounds?'

'No-one,' the boy replied.

'Where did you get them from anyway?'

There was a brief silence as the offenders looked at one another.

'We bought 'em, Mrs McDowell.' This time the second boy, who was not as bold as his friend, spoke with a slight quaver in his voice.

'Matthew, I don't believe Mr Findlay at the store would sell you cigarettes at your age.'

'We didn't get 'em from the store. We got 'em from old Miggles up on South Street.'

Mikaela shook her head.

'Who is old Miggles?'

'He has a scrap yard. He gives us cigarettes if we find him copper wire out of old engines.'

'I see,' Mikaela said sternly, trying to look as though she understood what on earth they were talking about.

'Please don't tell Mum,' Alex said, the formerly resolute chin dropping slightly. 'She'd bash me.'

Mikaela remained silent. What Alex said was possibly

true. Gareth had mentioned his domestic situation in the past. But smoking in the school grounds was absolutely banned, and the parents would have to be notified.

The third boy was looking rather green.

'I don't feel so good,' he managed to say.

'I'm not surprised, Paul. Smoking is a disgusting habit and makes you feel ill, not to mention the long-term effects of lung cancer. But no doubt Mr Lewis will give you a lecture on all that.'

At the mention of the principal's name, a visible shudder went through the boys. Mikaela had experienced the wrath of Gareth first hand, and she did not envy the students in their position at all. Part of her wanted to take each one in her arms and tell them it would be alright and that growing up was sometimes hard. But this was school and rules were rules. And the person to see when those rules were broken was Mr Lewis.

As she led the three students across the yard towards the principal's office, heads turned. The three were a sorry sight as they walked to face the consequences of their behaviour. Mikaela spoke to Gareth first, explaining the situation, then left the room to return to playground duty, thankful in this case that she was not the principal.

The midday sun was remarkably warm as she wandered across the oval, keeping an eye on the ball games that were in play. Further away across the highway stood the silos, their imposing figures dark against the sky. She was contemplating the silos when a yellow ute shot past her up the highway towards town. It gave a beep and the driver waved. Mikaela waved back with no idea who was inside, smiling at the friendliness of the townspeople in Turramore.

Two of Mikaela's grade one girls skipped up to her, grinning from ear to ear.

'Look what we found, Mrs McDowell.'

The child with long black pig tails held out her hand on which sat a large quivering stick insect.

'It thinks Lucy is a tree,' whispered the other child in awe.

'It does, Jessica,' Mikaela commented, trying hard not to show her distaste for large insects with the capacity to fly in your face.

'Can we keep it?' Lucy asked. 'We could put it in a bottle.'

'It might be a bit big.'

'What if we chopped its legs off?'

'I don't think so…'

'Can you hold it for us while we go to the toilet?' Jessica asked.

Mikaela took a deep breath. She was constantly amazed at how unafraid country girls were of things like spiders and beetles and stick insects. Most little girls in the city would have run a mile by now.

'How about you just sit it in the bushes until you get back?'

'But…'

Both girls suddenly shifted their gaze to a point behind Mikaela's shoulder, and at the same time she heard the sound of tyres on gravel. Turning she saw that the yellow ute which had driven past earlier had pulled up beside them on the other side of the school fence. The door opened and out stepped Zac Hamilton.

'Thought you looked hot out here,' he smiled, a cap pulled down to shield his eyes from the sun. The shadow from the cap made his tanned cheeks seem more hollow and emphasised the fine bone structure of his face. He handed her a can of cold lemon squash.

'Is this for me?' she asked, aware of the children's eyes on her.

'I got it just then at the cafe when I went to buy dinner. I thought you might need it, out here in the sun.'

'That's very kind of you,' Mikaela laughed. 'Are you working around here today?'

'South. Spraying some crops down towards Hillsford. I usually come back to Turramore for dinner, because they've got better pies here.'

He smiled and turned to the girls on the other side of the fence.

'What you got there?'

Lucy held out her hand, but remained silent.

'Hmm, a stick insect. I used to catch them when I was little. They're good fun.'

Lucy smiled back. Zac had made a fellow insect-loving friend.

'I'd better keep going. Sun'll be down early tonight.' He nodded towards her unopened can. 'Make sure you drink that.'

'I will. Thanks again.'

'I'll see you around. You too, girls.' And as he turned to go, he reached to touch Mikaela's arm lightly. She watched him get back into the yellow ute and the girls waved as he sped down the highway on his way out of town.

Mikaela opened the can of soft drink and took a slow sip. There was silence for a moment and then Jessica spoke.

'Was that your husband, Mrs McDowell?'

Mikaela coughed suddenly, choking on the fizzy liquid.

'Oh no, Jessica. No, he's just a friend.'

'He's nice,' commented Lucy in an innocent voice, stroking the stick insect.

Mikaela felt the lemon squash sting at the back of her throat and she suddenly had no desire to drink anymore of the sickly sweet liquid.

'Lunch time must be almost finished,' she murmured

and she led the girls and their stick insect back to the school building.

*****

After school had finished Mikaela sat with Gareth in the staff room, coffees in their hands, analysing the day's events.

'I rang Paul and Matthew's parents.' Gareth's voice was soft and his face looked rather haggard after the long day. 'They were shocked, which is no surprise. I think this cigarette-trading thing is only a recent development. As for Alex, his mother wasn't home, so I spoke to his grandmother. She seemed quite reasonable about it all.' He sighed deeply. 'I'm not sure what to do about it now. I guess this is a warning, and more serious consequences will take place if it happens again.'

Mikaela noted his tired eyes and the droop around the sides of his mouth.

'Are you okay?' she asked gently.

Gareth smiled at her.

'I'm okay, Mikaela. I'm getting old, that's all. I don't like to have to deal with these sorts of circumstances. I don't have the strength anymore. Must be time to retire, hey?'

Mikaela smiled back at the principal, and took a sip of her coffee. She had no words to offer him. Perhaps he was right. She had always imagined she would be teaching with him for years, but maybe that was just not going to happen.

'It's Friday night. Why don't you come and have tea with us?'

Gareth shook his head.

'It's good of you to ask me, but I think I'll just head home and get to bed early. I wouldn't want to disturb the newly married couple.'

He grinned at her and she returned the smile, putting the coffee mug to her lips and choosing once again to remain silent.

*****

The house was in darkness when she returned home. She ran down the cold hall and turned on a few lights then went to light the fire, hoisting a large Mallee root into the Coonara and prodding the embers to encourage the flames. Eventually the wood began to glow and flicker and she sat back on her haunches for a moment, the steel poker still in her hand, shifting little sticks that were lying at the edges of the fire. The sticks reminded her of Lucy's stick insect and she wondered what had been its eventual fate. She thought of Lucy's face when Zac had stopped to give her a drink. The girls had been so in awe. She laughed to herself and poked at the fire – Zac was certainly an interesting guy.

A sudden pop sent a spark out towards her and a piece of burning ember landed on her hand, causing her to flinch and brush it off quickly. She closed the door of the Coonara and hastily went into the kitchen to run some cold water over her hand. As the tap ran, she leant her forehead on the high cupboard, closed her eyes and tried to think of Thomas.

Chapter Twelve

Mikaela heard Thomas get out of bed, and listened to him moving about the room as he prepared for work. She opened one eye. It was so early that the sun was still struggling to peek through the bedroom window. She closed the eye and turned over in the bed, pulling the covers up to her chin. It was Saturday morning – people were meant to sleep in on Saturday mornings.

She must have dozed off again, because the next time she woke the sun had succeeded in feebly entering her bedroom. She could hear sparrows making a racket outside and knew there was no point in moping around in bed. She sat up slowly, reaching for her dressing gown and shoving her feet into the slippers that had been pushed under the bed. Yawning, her eyes fell upon the Bible under her lamp. She pondered it for a moment, laying her hand on the cover. She knew she should be reading it, reading God's promises and truths, but for some reason her motivation was poor, as it had been so much lately. She let her hand fall away from the leather cover, her heart heavy. It was going to be another long day.

She rambled through a breakfast of Weet-bix and toast, listening to the morning news on the radio, then made herself a coffee. She knew she should be doing something worthwhile, like planting a vegetable patch or painting a room, but just at the moment she felt quite useless and totally devoid of energy. She gazed out through the kitchen window, which looked out onto the fernery and the laundry block over to the side. She thought about the day when she and Bill had discovered the cellar, and a plan began forming in her mind. There was no point in hanging around at home. Thomas himself had suggested she should get out and see people. She would go to Elizabeth's and talk to Bill, and she would ask him about the copper house that he had mentioned the previous week.

An hour later the ute was roaring with its usual gusto, the engine rumbling under the bonnet as she warmed it up under the peppertree. When she was convinced it wouldn't stall on her, she took it down the driveway and out onto the road.

It was a beautiful morning, cold but very clear and bright, with no trace of the rain of last week. Maybe Thomas would finish the cropping today. She shook the thought from her head. The more she fretted over not seeing Thomas, the worse the day would get. It was better to think about other things, and put Thomas in the back of her mind.

She was nearing town when she noticed a man walking casually along the side of the road towards her. She knew it had to be Bill, and she laughed out loud. He had got away from Elizabeth again. She slowed as she came closer to him, and pulled the ute into the Mallee trees beside the bitumen. She saw Bill stop and look up, and then his face grinned at her from behind the thick glasses.

Mikaela jumped down from the driver's side and slammed the door shut behind her. The fresh morning air was cool on her face.

'Bill! Don't tell me you're out walking again?'

'Bill walking,' he beamed. He was perspiring heavily and seemed to be quite out of breath.

'Where is Elizabeth?'

'At the shop. Bill walk here from the shop.'

Mikaela shook her head.

'So you've walked all the way from town, Bill? Just as well I found you. How about you get in and I'll give you a lift? We'll go and find Elizabeth.'

Bill nodded happily, and went around to the passenger door. He stopped for a moment.

'Are you right, Bill?'

'Lynny open the door. Bill's arms hurt.'

Mikaela came around to the door.

'What's wrong with your arms, Bill?' Before he could answer, however, a noise startled them, a humming buzz from the sky. Mikaela looked up, squinting slightly in the sunlight, and saw the red and white plane. It was flying low and heading towards them. As they watched, it cleared a fenceline and dropped down gradually into the paddock beside them. Mikaela found herself catching her breath as the wheels of the plane touched down on the grassy ground, kicking up some dirt. The propeller whizzing, the plane taxied around slowly, coming to a stop not far from the road. In a moment, the pilot had opened the door and dropped down onto the earth.

'Look Bill, it's Zac.'

Bill's mouth had fallen open during the landing. Now he smiled as Zac, wearing a lightweight blue jacket and jeans, came sauntering towards the ute.

'I thought that was you travelling down the road,' Zac said with a smirk as he reached the pair. 'You met your uncle way out here?'

'Yes, he likes to walk,' Mikaela explained, smiling at Bill

who was still staring goggle-eyed at the plane. 'Do you normally land in paddocks? Or have you brought me another drink?'

'Yes to the first question, and unfortunately no to the second,' the pilot replied. 'We often land in paddocks, as long as they're flat, grassy and not too wet. It's just part of the job.'

'And how did you know this was my ute? It must look the same as a hundred others.'

'You learn to see a lot from the sky,' Zac explained with a grin. 'You just get to know things – I'll explain it to you one day.'

'Bill have a look?' Bill was pointing with a slightly shaky arm towards the plane.

'You want to have another look? Sure.'

Somehow Bill and Mikaela scrambled over the fence and walked with Zac over to the aircraft.

'It was such a great morning for flying. I left about six o'clock from Hillsford – it was magic.'

'I'll have to take your word for it, Zac,' Mikaela chuckled. 'I just don't think I would have the same sentiments if I was up there.'

'Too busy closing your eyes?'

'Something like that. My head in a sick bag, perhaps.'

'Maybe I'll take back my flying offer, in view of upholstery protection.'

They stood near the plane, watching Bill move around and under it, touching and tapping.

'He's fascinated,' Mikaela said quietly. 'Maybe he didn't realise it could fly when we saw it tied down at your aunt's house. How is you aunt, by the way?'

Zac shrugged, pushing his hands into his jacket pockets.

'I don't know. I haven't seen her since then. Once the weather cleared I was off back to Hillsford. Had to escape, you know.' She caught him looking at her and she smiled back, enjoying the conversation and the easy way he spoke to her.

'I felt a bit like escaping today,' she muttered, momentarily throwing caution to the wind.

'You did?'

'Just got a bit tired of looking at myself, so that's why I went out to visit Bill. I didn't realise he'd be on the road halfway to my house.'

They were silent for a moment, listening to the Mallee trees rustle behind them.

'You know, you can always call me, if you needed someone to talk to.'

Mikaela felt her heart jump slightly and she took a deep breath.

'That's nice of you, Zac, but how would I do that? You're buzzing around in that pretend bird all day.'

'I'll give you my phone number in Hillsford. Just leave a message and I'll come on up.'

Mikaela laughed nervously and wondered if Zac could sense her discomfort. At the same time, a little thrill had passed through her, bringing with it an immediate sense of guilt.

'You'll have to let me think on that one,' she smiled back.

'Have a talk to Thomas about it. I'm sure he'd understand.'

Had this man just arrived on the planet? Ringing Zac so that he could fly up for a cup of Earl Grey while Thomas was on the tractor – somehow Mikaela didn't think her husband would be too eager about that idea.

'I'd better get Bill back to town,' she said finally. 'Elizabeth will be worried.'

'I'm glad I was able to catch up with you again – twice in two days, that's pretty lucky. And it's good to see Bill too.

He's a nice sort of bloke.'

'He is,' Mikaela murmured, watching her uncle. He had wandered back towards the fence and was shuffling around the Mallee trees, picking up sticks and cracking them across his knee. All of a sudden he stopped dead still, the stick falling from his hand.

'What is it Bill? What can you see?'

For a moment, Bill didn't answer, then a single word escaped in a strangled way from his throat.

'Snake.'

'What did he say?' Zac asked.

'He said snake,' and Mikaela was already running over towards her uncle. 'It's alright, Bill, just don't go near it.'

'A snake? This time of year?' She heard Zac following behind.

'It's alright – it's dead,' panted Mikaela, seeing the half-rotten form lying amongst the fallen branches of the trees. 'Probably road kill.'

'Bill don't like snakes.'

'It's okay Bill, it's a dead one...' She turned to look at him, and with horror realised he had lost all colour in his face. 'Bill, are you alright?'

'Bill don't like snakes,' he repeated, his eyes large, sweat breaking out on his forehead and above his lip. And in the next moment he had turned and was running away from them, heading out across the paddock in a clumsy lopsided fashion.

'Bill! Wait!'

'What's the matter with him?' asked Zac.

'He has a paranoia about creepy crawly things, especially snakes. We've got to calm him down.'

She began to run after him, but as she watched, she saw him come to a slow stop ahead of them.

'Bill?'

Suddenly he was clutching at his chest and in the next instant he had toppled heavily sideways into the dirt.

Mikaela screamed his name and ran harder, reaching him in a moment and throwing herself to her knees beside him.

'Bill! Bill, what's the matter?'

'Sick blood...' her uncle gasped between pale lips.

'He's having a heart attack,' said Zac, breathing hard behind them. 'I'll get the ute.'

'Can't we use the plane?'

'There's only one seat. You stay here and talk to him.' Then Zac had left, running back towards the ute. Mikaela watched him for a moment. He would have to find a gate to bring the ute into the paddock – more wasted time. She turned back to Bill and loosened the shirt from around his neck, trying hard to remember her first aid skills. He was breathing fast, his hands still clasped to his chest, perspiration dripping down into his ears. His glasses had fogged up, so she took them off and gave them a quick wipe.

'Hurts, Lynny,' he whispered.

'I know, Bill.' She replaced the glasses, trying to be gentle even though her hands were shaking. 'Try not to speak. Zac's getting the ute and we're going to take you to the hospital, and there you'll feel all better.' She could feel her voice beginning to crack and her heart was pounding so hard she wondered if she was going to suffer the same fate.

'Bill likes Lynny.'

'I know. I like you too, Bill.' She could feel tears starting in her eyes, and she wiped at her face, annoyed that she could not be strong for him.

'Lynny go to the copper house. Don't forget the copper house.'

'Bill, for heavens sake, stop talking. You'll have to take me to the copper house yourself. You get all better, then you take me there.' Where the hell was Zac? This was all taking

125

far too long. What did the books say, that treatment needed to be started within an hour? They would hardly make it to Leighton in time.

There was a roar in the distance and the ute was coming towards them. Zac wheeled it around so that the passenger door was close to the fallen man. Somehow they managed to lift his heavy weight and struggled to push him into the seat. Zac got behind the wheel and Mikaela squeezed in beside Bill, allowing his body to slump against hers. It was uncomfortable and she felt like the breath was being squeezed out of her at every bump, but she put her own feelings out of her mind.

The journey to Leighton took forever. Mikaela had done a similar trip before, cradling Thomas in her arms who had been badly burnt.

'I hate this, I hate this,' she whispered over and over again, checking that Bill was breathing for the hundredth time. Trees and paddocks whizzed past endlessly. It had to stop eventually. It just had to stop.

It did stop. They tore into Leighton at a speed the ute had probably never done in its existence, and turned into the base hospital. Zac took the ute through the ambulance bay, hardly allowing it to stop before jumping out and yelling through the sliding doors. In a moment a stretcher had been rolled out and a team of paramedics were helping Mikaela and Bill out of the car. Bill was placed on the stretcher and wheeled into the emergency area, Mikaela and Zac following close behind.

A nurse stopped them from continuing into the curtained area.

'If you could wait out here, I'll get some details from you.'

'But…' began Mikaela.

'It's best to let the doctors have full concentration. Someone will be out soon to let you know how things have progressed. In the meantime…' She continued warbling on, but to Mikaela it was just background noise. All she could hear as she trained her eyes on the curtained area was Bill's voice, whispering his devotion to her as he lay struggling to breathe in the dirty paddock.

*****

It had been half an hour and they had heard nothing. They sat in the chairs of the emergency department, Mikaela slouched with her elbows on her knees, holding an empty paper cup. Even though she had finished the coffee she hadn't tasted a single sip – it had only been useful for warming up her frozen hands and body.

'I just can't believe this. This just can't be happening.'

Beside her Zac said nothing. Mikaela rubbed her hand over her eyes, suddenly feeling very tired.

'I can't even get on to Elizabeth. I've tried everybody – I don't know what else to do.'

'You've done all you can, Mikaela.'

'But somebody should be here.'

'I'm here.'

'I know, but…' She looked up at him, suddenly aware of the warmth of his nearness. 'I'm sorry, Zac. Of course you're here, and you've just been marvellous. I don't know what I would have done without you.'

'He'll be okay, Mikaela. Just wait and see. He'll be fine.'

'Do you think so?'

'Absolutely.' She felt his hand move over hers and he held her gaze for a moment. 'You don't need to worry about a thing.'

'Zac, he's not well. He has a heart condition and he's old and…I don't know if his body's going to be strong enough to deal with this.'

'There's nothing more you can do, Mikaela.'

His eyes did not shift from hers. For a long while she was frozen by the intensity of his gaze. Then very slowly his face moved towards her. She knew in a moment what was happening and she felt the coffee cup drop from her hands as she allowed herself to accept his slow kiss upon her lips. Inside, her world collapsed.

I will give you the treasures of darkness, riches stored in secret places, so that you may know that I am the Lord, the God of Israel, who summons you by name
Isaiah 45:3

Chapter Thirteen

The fine rain drizzled onto Mikaela's umbrella and dripped off the ends like slow monotonous tears. Her long black coat did little to stop the pervading wind from chilling her to the bone. The minister had closed his book and the coffin was being lowered into the muddy ground. A few people threw flowers into the grave as the wooden box disappeared from view.

'Did you want to put your flowers in, Mikaela?' Thomas' voice seemed to come from a long way off, even though he was right by her side. She looked down at the flowers in her hands, red carnations that were beginning to wilt from being clutched too tightly. Her legs felt heavy, but she managed to walk towards the ugly scar in the ground and toss in the scarlet offerings, watching them hit the hard casket at the bottom.

Pastor Richard said a final prayer, and then people began to quietly shift around, making soft comments to one another. Richard walked slowly towards Mikaela.

'How are you going?' His voice was gentle, and he placed his hand on her arm.

Mikaela shook her head.

'I don't really know. I feel like I'm in another world at the moment.'

'That's how it is sometimes. Reality doesn't set in for a few days, and then it comes in waves. I think it's God's way of allowing us to cope.'

'I'm not sure I know much of God's ways anymore.' She saw Richard look startled, but her emotions were so numbed from the events of the last week that she didn't care.

'We all feel like that sometimes, Mikaela. It doesn't mean He's not there.'

'I know.' She could say nothing more. Thomas came up beside her.

'Would you like to go now? People are coming back to Mum's for afternoon tea.'

Mikaela shook her head.

'I can't yet. I just want to walk for a while.'

'Would you like me to come with you?'

'No. I just want to be alone.' She felt tears sting her eyes. Thomas was being so considerate and gentle, and she was rejecting his support. But how could she accept love from someone that she had betrayed? Her punishment was to grieve alone.

She moved away from the gravesite and walked slowly towards the rear of the cemetery. She was aware of faces - Andy's, Gareth's - but she tried to keep her eyes down, taking note only of the dirt and grass. The ground was wet and sad, and the normally sweet smell of rain on the earth only served as a reminder to her that those buried under the earth would never smell rain again.

The doctors had said that nothing could have been done to save Bill. His heart was damaged even before the attack, and they were surprised that he had lived as long as he had. He had not suffered at the end, and he had been in the best of hands. They were all words that were meant to make her feel better, but in the end that's all they were – words. They did nothing to stop the incredible guilt eating away at her insides. Guilt that she had allowed Bill to continue his walking escapades, guilt that she hadn't been more vigilant in watching him as he was poking around the trees, guilt that she had allowed a virtual stranger to access her deeper emotions…

She had not seen Zac since the day they had spent at the hospital. Elizabeth and Helen had eventually arrived, and Zac had quietly taken his leave. She felt physically ill every time she thought of him, his kindness, his good-natured banter, his attractive looks…but also the way she had fallen under his spell at a time when she was an emotional mess. She had been lonely, and she had been afraid. He had seen her state of mind, and had taken advantage of her. Now she would have to live with the guilt of that moment for the rest of her life.

There was no way she could tell Thomas. What would her new husband think of her? How could she have made such a mess of her new life in the country? She sighed deeply and the air shuddered out of her in painful ripples.

She was aware of somebody coming up beside her. She turned to see Elizabeth, her fine hair pasted onto her head with the rain. Elizabeth gently placed her arm in the crook of Mikaela's and smiled, even though her forehead remained lined with worry.

'You know, Bill loved the rain. He would have thought this day was just right.'

Mikaela said nothing, and they walked in silence for a while, following the muddy track around the cemetery.

'There was nothing you could have done, Mikaela.'

'I know that, Elizabeth, people keep telling me.' Her voice

sounded sharper than she had expected, and she glanced up at the older woman. 'I'm sorry, I didn't mean to snap.'

'It's alright, honey. We've all been under a lot of strain. I just don't want you to blame yourself for what happened.'

Mikaela nodded wearily.

'I know. I just can't believe he's gone. I was just getting to know him. It seems so unfair.'

Elizabeth nodded.

'It does. Life's like that sometimes.' There was no simple explanation in her words, but her acceptance of the fact made Mikaela feel a little better. Maybe in time her grief regarding Bill would heal. Her guilt regarding Zac would never heal.

They passed the black marble headstone that showed Donald McDowell's final resting place, and paused for a moment. A question formed in Mikaela's head.

'Where are your parents buried? I haven't seen any headstones here with their names.'

'In an old cemetery way out off the eastern road. I would have liked Bill to have been buried there with them, but it's not in use anymore.'

'Do you think he would have minded not being buried back in Sydney?'

'He had no relatives in Sydney, and from what his carers told me, many of his close friends with Downs died years ago. He'll have a good deal more visits from people back here in Turramore, don't you think?'

Mikaela nodded.

'Well, I'll be here every week, for a start.'

Elizabeth smiled at her and patted her on the shoulder. As she did, a sudden thought entered Mikaela's mind.

'Carolyn – is she in the cemetery with your parents?'

'No,' Elizabeth said wistfully, 'Carolyn never came home. Her last wish was that her body be given for science – you know, research. It was something she had always wanted to do. Her belongings were sent home – I think Gareth has a few items, and I have a couple of things, but not much to speak of.'

Mikaela nodded and watched the rain trickle slowly down the headstone in front of them. Her connection with her natural mother was even more tenuous now that she knew there was no gravesite to visit. Her uncle had gone, her father was gradually succumbing to age – she knew she would have to hold on tightly to Elizabeth and Andy before all connections to her past hidden life were extinguished.

'I can't believe I never asked you that before,' she sighed. 'Not that it would have mattered anyhow. Some sort of memorial would have been nice though…'

'All we have is memories,' Elizabeth said softly, 'and I'm happy to share all of them with you.'

A third umbrella came close, and Thomas was beside Elizabeth.

'Are you ladies coming back to Mum's soon? It's getting pretty wet out here.'

'We're coming right now,' said Elizabeth, her voice chipper, 'aren't we, Mikaela?'

Mikaela forced a smile and nodded, and allowed Thomas and Elizabeth to escort her back through the cemetery.

*****

Helen's house was warm and dry, and the aroma of coffee was comforting. David and Emily were there, their arms around Mikaela as soon as she arrived. Richard's wife Amanda was helping Helen serve out drinks and plates of tiny sandwiches. Gareth was handing a cup of tea to Elizabeth. There were a few of Elizabeth's friends from the church and the school who had come to show their support. Mikaela tried to mingle and talk, but she felt tired and had a deep desire to go home and just crawl into bed.

Ian Scott arrived a little later with Andy, helping him through the doorway with his wheelchair. Andy grinned at Mikaela when he saw her, and they found a seat together beside a window. Outside the rain teemed.

'It's gonna be a good crop this year, with all this rain.'

'Great,' Mikaela commented, trying to sound positive.

'How are you coping with all the festivities?'

'Oh, alright I guess,' Mikaela smiled at his use of words. 'I'm looking forward to going home. I just want to fall asleep and wake up to find it was all a bad dream.'

'It's tough, Mik,' and Andy lowered his voice. 'Stuff like this, like what happened to Bill. But he was a different bloke when he spoke of you. His face would light up. It's great he got the chance to meet you.'

'We didn't get time to get to know each other, Andy.'

'Sure you did. You got to know him better than anyone. And what's more important, he got to know you.'

Mikaela thought about Andy's words for a moment.

'Okay, maybe he got to know me a bit, but what was that worth?'

'Everything. You reminded him of his sister, and he adored her. You made his last weeks very special, Mikaela.'

Mikaela said nothing, but sighed and fiddled with the sleeve of her jacket. She could feel Andy's eyes on her.

'And how's that Thomas bloke? Treating you alright, I hope?'

Her heart sped up slightly and her cheeks felt warm. It was a topic she wanted to avoid.

'Yeah…I guess so. He's been very busy.'

'That's hard, but cropping's over now. You guys will get to have some time to yourselves now. I'd better not pop in unannounced!' He grinned, but Mikaela could not meet his eyes. He was silent for a moment, and from the corner of her eye she could see his face change.

'Okay, what's going on?'

She took a deep breath. Was she really going to tell Andy what had been happening in her life?

'I made a mistake.'

'Yes…?'

'I let somebody too close to me and…I let him kiss me.' She closed her eyes and put her hand over her face. 'It's so embarrassing, and I feel really awful about it all.'

Andy said nothing for a moment, and she half expected him to turn his wheelchair around and leave her sitting by herself.

After a moment she heard him sigh.

'Well, it was one kiss. Does it matter? You haven't fallen in love with the guy?'

'No! Never. I don't have any feelings for him at all. It was just…I was lonely, he was there…do you know what I mean?'

'I think so,' he replied.

Mikaela wondered if he really did.

'So how did Thomas take it?' Andy asked.

Mikaela didn't reply, and her silence was her answer.

'You haven't told him, have you? Right, well there's the problem.'

'But I can't tell him, Andy. What will he think of me? He'll never trust me again. I don't even trust me.'

'I do. Circumstances have not been easy for you guys since you came back from your honeymoon. Things get rough, we make mistakes. It doesn't mean we are doomed for eternity. It just means we learn and we move on.'

Mikaela looked at Andy's sombre face and couldn't help but smile.

'Andy, you've gone all serious on me. I'm not used to that.'

'I'm a man of many talents, remember?' he replied.

'Okay, oh great man of wisdom, how do I 'move on'?'

'You start by telling Thomas.'

'He'll hate me.'

'Sure, for the first ten minutes. His ego will take a batter-ing. But then you've got to move him through that and come out on the other side.'

Mikaela shook her head.

'I don't know. 'Move through', 'other side' - it sounds like a freight train procedure. You don't know Thomas. He's going to have a melt down.'

'I do know Thomas, actually. And I've known him a little longer than you have. Tell him, Mikaela. There's no other way.'

There was movement at the doorway and Helen welcomed someone else into the house, rain dripping from his jacket.

'That's him,' Mikaela whispered, watching Zac remove his sodden coat and leave it beside the door. 'I was hoping he wouldn't show up today.'

'Zac Hamilton? You kissed Zac Hamilton?'

'Shh!'

'Well, I think you could have picked someone better than him. Like me, for example.'

'Andy, would you keep your voice down?'

'But then, that's right, I'm your cousin. Could get messy... yuck...'

'For goodness sake...!'

They watched as Zac walked casually into the living area and was offered a cup of tea by Amanda.

'How do you know him anyway?' Mikaela whispered, cringing as she watched Thomas come across the room to greet Zac.

'High school. He was thin and scrawny and used to get teased a lot. His dad was pretty strange too.'

'So I've heard.' Thomas was smiling and shaking Zac's

hand. Everyone knew that he had been instrumental in getting Bill up to the hospital. Nobody had asked why he had been with Bill and Mikaela in the first place. Mikaela didn't even know herself.

'I can't watch this. It makes me feel ill.' She glanced around quickly. 'I'm going to sneak out the back door. If you see Thomas, tell him I'm walking home.'

'You can't walk all that way.'

'Bill did.' She patted Andy's hand. 'Thanks for the talk,' and then she moved quickly out to the kitchen and through the back door.

Two old umbrellas stood propped against the back step. Mikaela took one and opened it over her head. Her own umbrella was at the front door and she didn't want to risk being seen by Zac. She would borrow Helen's and return it as soon as possible. She walked quickly through the wet backyard and opened the back gate, which led out onto the dirt track running behind the houses. The ground was muddy and sloshy, but Mikaela had dress boots on, so her feet were able to stay dry, even if they were slightly uncomfortable.

She tramped down the track, squelching in the puddles, lifting up the hem of the long black coat. It hadn't been that long ago that she had tramped down a similar track not far from here in her wedding dress, Erin's jacket held over her head. That special day seemed so long ago. Did it even happen at all or was it in a dream? These days it was hard to tell.

She came to the end of the track and turned westward. Across the road she could see the little school residence where she had lived for over a year. They had been hard days in a new town, but things had seemed a lot more innocent back then. Her character had grown and matured, as had her faith. She wondered whether she would grow or mature through her current battles – she doubted it.

She continued westward for a little way, then dog-legged past a few more houses and a large shed, until finally she saw the little bridge up ahead where the town road met the country road heading west out to McDowell Hill. She wondered how far along the road she would get before Thomas would discover she had gone and would come to pick her up in the ute. She longed for him to find her so that they could be close again.

She didn't have to wonder for much longer, because as she reached the bridge the sound of a utility engine came up behind her. She slowed as the vehicle pulled up beside her, turning her head to smile at the man behind the wheel.

But the ute did not belong to Thomas. It was a murky yellow, and the smile faded from her face as she recognised Zac in the driver's seat. He reached across and opened the passenger door.

'What are you doing out here in the rain?' he smiled. 'Hop in and I'll give you a lift home.'

She hesitated. The rain was actually becoming quite heavy and she was getting very wet. It would look ridiculous if she were to continue walking, but at the same time she didn't want Zac to get any more ideas about their relationship.

'Zac, we need to talk,' she offered through the doorway, rain dripping from her umbrella onto the passenger seat.

'Sure,' he shrugged. 'Just get in before you drown.'

She scrambled inside, shaking off the umbrella as she folded it and placed it at her feet. Then Zac put the vehicle into gear and they continued out along the Turramore West road.

'Can't believe this rain. I won't be flying for a few days. What did you want to talk about?' He sounded casual and at ease, and Mikaela wondered for a moment why she had felt she had needed to get away from him so quickly.

'About the other day, at the hospital. When you and I…

140

you know…'

'I enjoyed that moment. Didn't you?'

'No.'

He raised his eyebrows, still watching the road.

'You didn't? Then why did you kiss me back?'

Mikaela's stomach churned.

'I didn't kiss you back…I mean, I didn't mean to kiss you at all. I wasn't thinking.'

'I thought you were thinking quite well. You seemed very much in control.'

Mikaela kept her eyes ahead, watching the windscreen wipers attack the rain on the glass. None of her words seemed to be getting through to the man beside her. She wished they would arrive at McDowell Hill.

'Zac, I'm married. I have a wonderful husband, and it's not right to flirt with someone else. Surely you can see how wrong I've been.'

'Mikaela, you have done nothing wrong. It's your life. How you spend it and who you spend it with is totally up to you.'

'Not entirely…'

'What are you saying?'

'I have morals, Zac. I live by certain rules, one of which is faithfulness to my husband.'

'Don't let religion fool you, Mikaela. Religion doesn't have answers – it just produces more questions. Religion confuses people.'

Mikaela remained silent. The conversation was not going as she had expected. Now her faith had been brought into the equation, and she wasn't sure where she stood on that either.

The road rose slightly and the homestead emerged from the rain. Zac slowed the ute, and turned into the driveway, coming around the peppertree to pull up at the front gate. He turned the engine off and the cabin was filled with the sound of pure rain hitting the roof. She heard him sigh.

'Look, Mikaela, all I know is I think you are very beautiful and I also think you are very lonely. I don't think it's fair that you have to live all the way out here without any company. People go crazy in the bush – believe me, I know.' He reached over and took her hand before she had time to realise what he was doing. 'You don't have to tell anyone. It can become our little secret. We'll spend some time together, get to know each other better. You'll enjoy it, I promise. I'll make you happier than you've ever been.'

His hand was warm, but she felt the blood draining from her skin until her fingers were icy. Suddenly she needed to get out of the cabin, out into the rain, where she could be washed clean of the sinfulness that she felt was knocking at her door. She withdrew her hand and gathered up her umbrella, opening the door and jumping down to the ground outside in one movement. She looked back up into the ute where Zac was watching her.

'I'll come by and see how you're doing,' he was saying, his eyes dark and unswerving.

'No. Don't visit me anymore, Zac. I'm not interested – please understand me.'

'I can't understand you,' he replied quietly, 'especially when I know what you like and what you need. We'll work it out together – you'll see.' He started up the engine as she slammed the door shut and ran through the front gate. She heard the ute roar away up the driveway as she stumbled through the back door. Flinging the umbrella onto the kitchen table, she ran sobbing to her bedroom.

Chapter Fourteen

Somehow Mikaela managed to struggle through the remainder of the school week. Her thoughts were in a whirl, spinning from Zac to the day at the hospital to Thomas and then back again. Not being able to see her husband during her workdays made it somewhat easier to deal with her nagging guilt, and she feigned exhaustion in the evenings, taking herself to bed early so that she wouldn't have to converse at length with him. She knew that what she was doing was wrong and was in no way going to help the situation, but facing Thomas with the truth just seemed too difficult. Maybe there would be a 'right time' to tell him – then again, maybe there wouldn't.

On Saturday Thomas came through the kitchen door with blood smeared across the front of his shirt.

'What have you done?!' Mikaela cried, her brief life with him flashing before her eyes.

'Nothing,' he smiled. 'Dave's brought a sheep over for us and I've just hung it in the meat room. We're going to cut it up and put it all in the freezer.'

'Oh, that sounds…lovely. Did David kill it?'

'Yes. Do you think you could package it up as we go?'

'I guess so. How did he do it?'

'Never you mind. I'll take you to a sheep slaughter one day. Not during the first year of our marriage though.' He rifled through a cupboard at the back of the kitchen.

'Here we go,' and he tossed a carton of plastic freezer bags onto the table. 'You can use those. Just make sure you get most of the air out before you tie them.'

He started back out the door.

'And by the way, you'd better wipe down the table with some disinfectant before we start. That's what Mum always did.' Then he left to go outside.

The whole table? Just how much meat was going to be coming in from the meat room? The 'room' was in actual fact a huge concrete pipe, sitting on its end and with a roof attached. It had been positioned further north of the laundry block, and had a door in each side to allow the breeze to flow through the room, keeping it cool for the meat. Mikaela had looked inside it once, noting the enormous steel hooks hanging from the roof and the blood stains on the floor. It had given her the shudders.

She began to dutifully wash and disinfect the table and then took some freezer bags out of the carton. At the last minute she put on a pair of disposable gloves that she had under the sink. She was vaguely aware of the electric buzzing noise of a saw in the distance, and after a few more minutes Thomas came in with a tray stacked high with chops, moist with blood.

'First load,' he said as he dumped the meat onto the table and retreated from the kitchen with the tray. Mikaela counted out the chops and began putting a few in each bag, trying to calculate how many they would eat at one time. She hadn't finished the first pile when Thomas came in with a second tray load.

'Some neck chops in this lot. Really sweet meat.'

'Neck chops – what do you do with those?'

'They're good for casseroles.' And he was gone again. Mikaela continued to work with the slippery red meat, blood beginning to ooze across the table. By the time Thomas brought in the third lot of meat, she was well behind.

'Here are some flaps.'

'I beg your pardon?'

'Rib flaps. They're good for roasting. Not much meat on them, but the bones are great to chew.'

'Thomas, I seem to be having some difficulty keeping up, and it's all a bit…well, 'bloody' is really the only word that fits. Can you slow it down a bit?'

'Not really. David's on a roll, and there's no stopping him when it comes to cutting up a sheep. You'll be right. I'll be in to help in a little bit.' He left again.

Mikaela reached for another plastic bag, her gloved fingers dripping with blood and slipping over the plastic opening. She dropped a chop, which fell heavily, spattering red gore across the floor. Annoyed she picked up another one, which did exactly the same thing. She stopped for a moment and wiped away a strand of hair that had fallen across her face.

'There's got to be a better way to do this,' she muttered. After a minute, she took off the gloves and pulled out a number of baking trays from under the oven. Then she found a roll of sandwich paper and pulled off sheets that were the same size as the trays. Gradually she began to layer the chops on to the trays with the paper between each layer. By the time Thomas came back in, she had almost finished.

'Shanks for soup, shoulders for roasting…' He stopped and raised his eyebrows at the layers of meat on the trays.

Mikaela explained.

'This is a whole lot easier. We freeze them like this first, then we bundle them into big bags. We can just pick out what we want as we go, because each piece will be individually frozen. It's a lot less messy too.'

Thomas nodded slowly in approval.

'Good idea, Miss City Girl. I think meat packaging suits you.'

'Terrific,' she muttered. 'How often do we have to do this?'

'It'll take us a long time to get through all this meat. Don't worry - we wont have to do it again for a while.'

'I'm guessing then that we are required to eat this sheep every night for the next year?'

'That's why they call it the old 'three hundred and sixty-five'.' He narrowed his icy blue eyes. 'Anyway, I thought you liked mutton?'

'Lamb. I like lamb. Mutton I'm not too sure about.'

Thomas smiled warmly at her and ran the back of his hand lightly over her hair.

'You'll get used to it, like everything else in this strange place.' He hesitated for a moment, Mikaela very aware of his closeness. 'Are you okay here, Mikaela? I haven't really spoken to you properly for a while.'

Now was certainly not the right time to be talking like this. Mikaela felt annoyance rise up in her - they were busy working, surrounded by blood and mess. There was still a lot to do. Why was Thomas asking her questions that she just couldn't answer? She turned to busy herself with the plastic bags, tidying them quickly.

'I'm okay here, Thomas,' she replied crisply.

'Good...' His voice trailed off. There was an awkward silence that spoke volumes.

David came into the kitchen, startling them both.

'How's it going in here? You look very organised, Mikaela.'

'Yes, I think I've conquered sheep packaging.' She picked up the box of plastic bags and went to the sink to get a cloth for the table, aware of Thomas' eyes on her. 'Did you enjoy cutting the poor animal up?'

'You don't think of it as something that was alive. You just think of it as the Sunday roast. Did you want to keep the tongue and the brains too?'

Mikaela stopped on her way back to the table and screwed up her face.

'Thanks all the same, David, but I don't think I could bring myself to eat something an animal's been thinking with or talking with.'

'Talking with?' repeated Thomas.

'Baaing, I think she means,' David added. 'No problem. I'll clean up out here and be on my way. Hope you enjoy the meals!'

He left them in the kitchen, Mikaela finishing up the table, and Thomas putting the trays and bags into the freezer.

'It was good of Dave to bring that sheep over for us,' he said casually.

'Yes,' Mikaela agreed, rinsing out the cloth and tidying the sink. She wanted Thomas to go back to work, so that she didn't have to feel the pressing need to tell him what had been happening to her.

'So…you didn't mind doing that job?'

'No, Thomas, I didn't mind at all.'

She turned to look at him. He was still standing beside the freezer, his face puzzled.

'Are you sure you're okay? You've been a bit…quiet, I guess. Is it something at work?'

Mikaela shook her head.

'No, I'm fine.'

'You know, you don't have to work. I can earn enough money to-'

'It's not work, Thomas,' she replied sharply. For a moment her confession lay hanging from her lips, then she sucked it back inside. 'I told you, I'm fine.'

This time the air between them was prickly. Thomas finally shrugged and moved to the door.

'Alright then. I'll go and clean out the meat room.' The kitchen door slammed behind him with a bang.

Mikaela flung the wet cloth into the sink.

*****

An hour later she was hanging out the washing. It seemed totally ridiculous, as the air was too cold for any effective drying to occur, but it had to be done and once again it was a way of passing the time. The cold garments flapped annoyingly in her face as she pegged them up, and it was probably the fact that her vision was partially obscured that she didn't notice Zac until he was almost under the clothesline itself. She gasped and dropped a handful of pegs.

'I'm sorry I startled you,' he smiled, his dark eyes flashing. 'Now your pegs will be all dirty.' He helped her pick them up and place them back into the bucket, which hung from the trolley.

'What are you doing here?' Mikaela asked, her voice slightly strained. She glanced instinctively behind him, looking for Thomas.

'The weather's cleared so I'm heading out today. I've got to do a few spray runs, then I'll be back later in the month. I came to ask you if you'd considered our plan.'

Mikaela swallowed hard. The air was suddenly freezing around her.

'What plan?'

'You and me, Mikaela. You need some time off. I'll come

148

by and pick you up, and we can go somewhere nice. Just tell Thomas you're visiting Mummy.'

At the mention of her mother, a sickening revulsion rose up in Mikaela.

'What are you talking about? Get out of here, Zac. I don't want anything to do with any of this.'

'Don't mess with me, Mikaela. I know what you want. You made it quite clear that day at the hospital.'

Mikaela stared at the man in front of her. His eyes were fiercely intense and a thin line of sweat had broken out above his upper lip. The veins in his neck were more visible than she had ever noticed before. He was changing before her eyes.

'Zac, I don't think I know you,' she whispered. 'I thought you were an understanding person, that you would understand my reasons for not wanting to pursue this thing. But you're not like that at all. What is your problem?'

'I don't have a problem, not a problem in the world, except that you are refusing an offer any other girl would take without hesitation.'

'Well maybe I'm not 'any other girl'. I'm Thomas McDowell's wife.'

In an instant he had closed in on her and had grabbed her wrist, his fingers tightening around it with ferocity. She gasped as pain shot through her arm.

'Thomas McDowell – you don't know a thing about Thomas, do you? You don't know that he was a bully at school, a brutal bully who mistreated innocent boys like me.' His face was close to hers and she felt moisture on her skin as he spat out the words.

'I don't know what you're talking about. Let go of me!'

'Hasn't Thomas told you about the day he buried me?'

'Buried you?'

'He and his mates dug a trench at the back of the school,

where no-one could see. They threw me in and covered the top with a sheet of corrugated iron. They left me in there with a piece of smoking Mallee root for good measure. After the dirt went on the top of the tin, there was no way out.'

Mikaela was silent, feeling the blood rushing past her ears with a noise like wind, her breathing fast and shallow.

'I could have died in there...' Zac's face came even closer to hers. 'That was the day my father was hit by that bloody train.'

'Zac, get away, I can't...'

Zac pulled harder on her wrist.

'It was the day my father died, Mikaela. And I wasn't at the hospital to say good-bye to him. I wasn't there, because they couldn't find me.'

He stared at her with his crazed eyes. She felt her arm beginning to ache from the downward pressure at her wrist.

'Zac, I'm sorry. I'm sure he didn't know what he was doing.'

'Oh he knew, alright. He knew exactly what he was doing. And if it wasn't for a teacher who found me, I might be there to this day.'

Mikaela's mind whirled in confusion and pain. The story sounded so unreal and so unlike the Thomas she knew. But kids could be cruel...

'If you let go of my arm, maybe we could talk about this properly.'

Just at that moment a noise came from the front of the house – it was the gate shutting. Thomas was coming in for dinner.

Zac leaned towards Mikaela, his breath hot across her mouth, his lips a fraction from hers.

'Remember, this is our little secret Mikaela. I'll come back. We'll go away together, just you and I. Then Thomas will understand what it's like to lose someone you love.'

In a moment he had gone, heading across the yard to jump the fence and run up towards the dirt road behind the house, where no doubt he had parked his ute. Mikaela leaned against the clothesline, rubbing her aching wrist, her knees quivering, her breath coming out in rasping sounds. The breeze chilled her but her armpits were wet with perspiration. She could hear Thomas in the laundry, washing his hands. She knew now there was no more time for secrets - she had to tell him everything.

*****

She had lit the fire to heat up the house, and now she and Thomas were seated in front of it, letting the warmth of the flames infuse their frosty bones. Thomas had eaten dinner while Mikaela had silently tidied the kitchen, her appetite gone. She had put on her watch to cover the red marks that were developing around her wrist.

Now she looked over at Thomas, the firelight flickering across his face. Zac had frightened her. His behaviour was bizarre and unnatural and it was no longer something she could handle on her own. Thomas needed to know what was going on.

Sadness welled up inside her as she studied her husband's face. How could she ever have looked for comfort in anyone else? How would Thomas ever forgive her for her stupidity?

'Thomas, there's something I need to tell you.' The words were out and her heart had started to race.

His eyes looked across at her, his lips smiling and relief showing on his face.

'I thought there might have been. What's been bothering you, Mikaela girl?'

She breathed heavily.

'It's not good. You're not going to be happy. But it was

a one-off, and I didn't know what I was doing.'

The smile began to fade.

'You're scaring me…'

'Don't be scared, Thomas,' and she reached out towards him. The strain of the last weeks welled up inside her. 'It was just one kiss, at the hospital. I didn't mean it, I was all emotional and frightened and I just let Zac kiss me. I'm sorry.'

It was out. Her mouth felt dry, and her heart was pounding.

'Zac Hamilton? You kissed him? I was talking to him at the funeral…' His voice trailed off, and he looked away. When he looked back at her, his eyes were filled with tears.

'Why, Mikaela? Am I not good enough anymore?'

'It's not that, Thomas. It's nothing like that. I don't have any feelings for the man, it was just the moment. There are no excuses, I know.'

Thomas shook his head as he looked at her, then slowly got up from his seat, wandering as if in a daze towards the doorway.

'I've got to go,' he muttered, and he disappeared into the kitchen. In a moment she heard the kitchen door slam.

She stayed slumped on the carpet, watching the flames behind the glass jumping in a bizarre dance of mockery. The tears fell in streams from her eyes and over her face. She curled herself into a ball, and sobbed uncontrollably.

She must have fallen into a half-sleep, because when she opened her eyes, the sun seemed to have shifted and the shadows in the room were different. She could hear a sound, faint over the crackle of the fire, but gradually becoming louder, and she realised that it was the sound that had woken her. Suddenly it became deafening, and she lifted her head as the roar of a plane's engine shook the glass in the window frame. She pressed her hands over her ears and saw the wheels of an aircraft loom over the verandah, and then somehow the plane had cleared the house and was climbing again into the eastern sky.

Sobbing, she began to rock back and forth, still holding her head in her hands. Then she cried out to her God.

Chapter Fifteen

The crops were coming up, millions of tiny bright green shoots poking up through the dark earth, transforming the paddocks into a glorious sweep of emerald. The early morning was crisp and sunny, and the air smelt fresh and pure.

Mikaela stood beside the paddock fence with her ute idling nearby, ready to drive to school. The countryside was turning into a magical place of beauty and she so wanted to enjoy the prettiness of her home amid the green paddocks, but a cloud remained over her life and her emotions. She watched Thomas in the distance, putting up a new part of the fence, his back bent over as he worked, his hair bright in the sunshine. He had said little to her over the past few days. They had gone to bed in silence and in the mornings he had left early. Mikaela went to work at the school, going through the motions of teaching and marking homework, doing playground duty and writing up lesson plans. There was no soul in anything she did. She knew her soul was grappling to survive under a heavy burden of guilt and confusion. Gareth asked her one lunch hour if there was anything wrong, but her tongue had felt like lead and she could not bring herself to tell him her troubles.

She kicked at the old fencepost beside her. One day it too would need to be replaced, just as Thomas was replacing the fence on the other side of the paddock. New for old, getting rid of the worn and damaged posts and replacing them with clean strong ones. The old post reminded her of herself - worn and damaged.

She had started to pray again. She had also picked up her Bible and opened it to the Psalms, reading the words of David as he cried out his anguish to God. She had not read those precious words for so long. What on earth had she been thinking, that now she was married she no longer needed the nutrition of the Bible and the fellowship of her Lord? She wondered where Thomas was in his spiritual growth. It was another area they hadn't spoken about.

She took a deep breath and turned to get into the ute. As she did she noticed waterdogs in the sky to the east. Perhaps a change was on the way.

The school day passed uneventfully but she was tired by the time she drove home again in the afternoon. When she reached the McDowell Hill gates, however, she hesitated. She hadn't heard Zac's plane lately and he had said he was going to be away working. She let the ute idle for a moment. She wondered if Mrs Hamilton had any light to shed on the situation Mikaela was now in. She put the ute into gear and continued west, leaving McDowell Hill behind.

The view of the paddocks on either side of her was magnificent and took her breath away. She rolled the window down and breathed in the cold air. The sun was low and the green wheat shimmered in the late afternoon light, like a green sea with rippling waves. All the work that Thomas had put in over the cropping period was paying off, and with the rain, it was looking like it might be a bumper harvest. She felt a slight twinge of regret that she hadn't been more supportive of his efforts when they had come home from their Tasmanian holiday. Thomas was a farmer – of course he would know when the work had to be done. This was the country. There was no nine till five around here; it was get the work done when the weather allowed it. That was what Thomas had done, and they would reap the rewards. Maybe she was slowly coming to see that.

Today she felt surprisingly calm about the situation with Zac. She had told Thomas the truth – at least most of it – and had asked for his forgiveness. She had told Zac plainly that she wanted nothing to do with him or his strange delusional 'plans'. She had prayed and prayed about it all, which she should have done at the very start. Now she had detached herself from her emotions and was willing to wait for her life to get back into some sort of order. She would make sure she learnt some important lessons from the whole sordid mess.

Even so, as she turned into Mrs Hamilton's drive, she felt nervous. She remembered her first strange meeting here. She pulled the ute to a halt, got out and went to the front door, ringing the rusted bell.

It took a while for the door to open, and then it only opened a crack.

'Yes? Who is it then?'

'It's Mikaela McDowell.'

'What do you want?'

'I just wanted to say hello, that's all.'

There was hesitation behind the door and then it was slowly opened. Mrs Hamilton stood there, her grey hair a tangled mess on top of her head, her left eye black and swollen, her face bruised completely down the left side. Mikaela sucked in her breath involuntarily and the two women looked at one another in silence for a moment.

'Yer come at a bad time. I ain't cleaned up the place yet.'

'It's no bother. We can talk out here if you like.' Mikaela was trying not to stare. 'What…happened to your eye?'

'Walked into the rake handle. It was leanin' on the back door.'

Again the silence surrounded them. Mikaela met the older woman's gaze.

'Are you sure it was the rake handle?'

'That's what I said, ain't it?'

'Well, did you get some ice on it? Should you be seeing a doctor?'

'It's nothin' that hasn't happened before…' muttered the stern-faced woman. 'I can look after meself.'

'I can take you if you like, to see Dr Warren.'

'Leave it, girl.'

Mikaela drew a quick breath.

'He had no right to hit you, Bonnie…'

'I said leave it. Leave it well alone.' The door was being closed as she spoke. The final words were hissed out through the crack. 'Get away from him, or you might be next.' The door shut quickly and Mikaela was left alone on the front porch.

*****

Bonnie Hamilton's words rang in Mikaela's head for the remainder of the week. The image of the woman's black and mangled eye haunted her in her sleep, and she realised that her fear of Zac had suddenly increased. The picture she was forming of the man was becoming more and more uncanny. He was violent, that was obvious. He had some vendetta against Thomas that involved an incident Thomas had never mentioned. He had a strange attraction to her, which seemed vastly disproportionate to the time they had spent together or the one kiss to which she had accidentally succumbed. Something was very wrong with Zac Hamilton – that fact alone was becoming clear.

On Friday afternoon, Mikaela stayed back at the school after the final bell to finish off a few jobs. Helen McDowell had invited her and Thomas for tea, so Mikaela had decided to come over straight from school. Helen had been struggling with a flu virus for a few weeks, and had put herself into isolation in case she spread the germs. Now she was back on her feet and trying to make up for lost time.

Mikaela arrived at Helen's house as the sun was touching the western horizon, her heart heavy and her spirit tired. Thomas arrived a little later and Mikaela watched him through the front windows as he got out of the red ute. He was looking tired too after the long week, and this week had certainly felt much longer than normal. Mikaela wondered if Helen would notice that things were strained between the two newlyweds.

The roast was delicious as it always was at Helen's house. Thomas did not say very much but was polite and reserved. Mikaela remembered when she had first met him, and how he was often in a reserved mood. She hoped that Helen would not see anything unusual about his behaviour.

Helen was, however, Thomas' mother, and nothing could escape her watchful eye. She brought the subject up as Mikaela was helping her do the dishes later in the evening. Thomas had ventured outside with a torch to have a look at a piece of guttering that was coming away from the house. Helen was obviously good at choosing her moments.

'Thomas looks worn out, Mikaela. Has he been overdoing things on the farm?'

'He has been very busy,' Mikaela replied. 'I haven't seen a lot of him lately.' What she said was true enough, but she didn't want Helen to know any further details.

'He needs to have a break. Get him off that farm and take him away for a day.'

'I'll mention it to him.'

'You're both working your fingers to the bone - you won't know each other soon. I've seen it happen before. But there I go, speaking where it's not my place...'

Mikaela put a dish on the draining board. Her mother-in-law was closer to the truth than she realised.

Thomas came in through the back door, taking off his coat and replacing the torch on a hook.

'It's cold out there,' he muttered, blowing on his hands. 'I'll get some tools and fix that gutter tomorrow, Mum.'

'Don't do it tomorrow. Goodness knows, it can wait. Get away somewhere, have some time off. I've just been telling Mikaela you both should spend some time together away from that farm.'

She busied herself into the living room, leaving Thomas and Mikaela alone in the kitchen.

'Did you tell her?' Thomas asked. It was the first time he had looked properly at her since the previous weekend.

'No. She's just perceptive.'

Mikaela pulled up her sleeves and took off her watch, taking over her mother-in-law's place at the sink. Thomas picked up a tea towel.

'She's right, we should get away. We need to talk.' He was gazing down at the tea-towel as he spoke.

'Are you ready to talk yet? Take all the time you need, Thomas. I'm the one at fault here. I take all the blame.'

'I've been thinking about that, Mikaela.' He absent-mindedly began to dry a glass. 'I don't think all the blame is yours. I haven't been a very attentive husband.'

He dried another glass in silence and Mikaela continued to wash. Eventually he spoke again.

'I should have been making you feel like you are the queen

160

of my life and my house – which you are. But I forgot my responsibilities. It's no wonder you looked for support in someone else.'

'Thomas, it wasn't like that…' she began.

'What is that?' His voice was sharp and startled her.

'What?'

'That – on your arm.'

She had forgotten that the dark bruising Zac had left around her wrist was still visible, and had extended slightly up her arm. She had been able to hide it so well under her long jumper sleeves and her watch. Now as she washed the dishes it was very distinct.

'It's nothing,' she murmured, fingering the dark skin. An image of Bonnie came to her, her eye blackened and her face bruised. 'Actually, Zac did it.'

'What?' Thomas' face was incredulous.

'He came over that day we did the meat. He threatened me – I didn't want to tell you. I thought you would worry.'

Thomas let the tea-towel drop to the bench and reached for his wife's arm.

'You must be joking. You're saying that Zac Hamilton grabbed you so hard that he caused this?' He cradled her arm in his hand, running his fingers gently along the ugly flesh, but when he looked up at her, his eyes were as hard as steel. 'Where the hell have I been? Why haven't I seen this before?'

'Thomas, don't do this. It's not your fault. I was scared of what you might think.'

'I know what I think, Mikaela. I think Zac Hamilton needs to be shot for doing this to my wife.'

'His aunt fared worse,' Mikaela murmured quietly. They stood together in the kitchen, both looking at the wound and each other.

'Tomorrow I'll take you out to the dam,' Thomas whispered suddenly. 'We'll take the bike, and we'll go yabbying. We'll talk, and you can tell me everything that has happened, from the very beginning.'

'I'd like that,' Mikaela whispered and she gently rested her head against her husband's chest.

Chapter Sixteen

S aturday morning dawned clear and cold. The sun shone brilliantly and it was a perfect winter's day in the Mallee. Mikaela dressed in jeans and a warm jumper and jacket, and fished out her gloves. Coming out onto the front porch of the house, she could hear a motorbike engine roaring into life in one of the sheds. A moment later, Thomas was riding up towards the house, denim jeans hugging the body of the bike and his old black leather jacket gleaming softly in the sun. Mikaela knew that the bike existed, but she had never seen Thomas ride it. The vision of him slung across the thudding machine took her breath away. He beckoned her over with a smile, and she shouldered the knapsack he had prepared and ran down through the gate.

He helped her up behind him, and she wrapped her arms around his warm body.

'Hang on!' she heard him yell above the noise of the engine, and suddenly they were off, cruising down the driveway. They slowed as they came to the road, then took off to the other side, through an open gateway, and across the green paddock.

It felt like they were flying. Thomas revved the bike into a higher gear, and they tore over the ground. The cold wind was bracing in Mikaela's face and her hair flew out behind her in all directions. The sky was broad and blue and they were escaping into a glorious day. Mile after mile of ground seemed to disappear under the wheels. Mikaela smiled and hung on tightly to her man, feeling very safe.

After a little while the ground changed, and the crop gave way to bare dirt. The bike slowed and eventually Thomas brought it to a stop under a group of gum trees not far from a large dam. Mikaela alighted awkwardly.

'That was excellent,' she breathed, feeling her face flushed from the cold wind.

'It's a good feeling, isn't it,' agreed Thomas, taking the knapsack from her back. 'I guess I should have given you a helmet, but to tell you the truth I don't think we've ever owned one. The bike's only used on the farm.'

'I guess that's a country thing,' smiled Mikaela. 'In the city you'd get fined for not wearing a helmet.'

Thomas pulled a plastic container from the sack, along with some string. He took the lid off the container and Mikaela wrinkled her nose at the rancid meat inside.

'I hope that's not lunch.'

'No, but hopefully it's a way of catching lunch. I'm going to tie a bit of meat onto the end of some string and throw it out into the dam. If the yabbies are there, they'll soon sniff it out. Then we'll pull them in with the yabby net.'

'And what is a yabby net? Is that in your sack as well?'

'No, the yabby net should be…' he walked over to a group of Mallee trees further along from the dam, '…here.' Reaching up into one of the branches, he pulled out a long pole with a flat net made of chicken wire at one end. It looked like an oversized tennis racquet.

'We've always kept this hanging in the tree for yabbying days, along with the bucket.' He produced a dirty looking plastic bucket from another branch.

Mikaela helped him tie the meat onto lengths of string and they dropped each length a few metres out into the dam. After a short while, Thomas instructed Mikaela to slowly drag each piece of string in, while he got ready with the net. Once he sighted the yabbies around the meat, he began to flick them quickly up onto the bank.

They looked like large grey prawns.

'Quick, grab them before they get back into the water.'

'But they've got claws!'

'Just get them around the back.'

They gathered up as many as they could from each net 'flick', until they eventually had a bucketful. The creatures moved and twisted in their confined environment.

'Poor things,' Mikaela commented as she peered into the bucket.

'Now don't go getting all sentimental about yabbies. They're good eating – that's all you need to know.'

'But Thomas, look at them all. They have no idea what's about to happen to them.'

'And just as well, or we might have a yabby riot on our hands.' He laughed at Mikaela and shook his head. 'You're a funny bird. How about I show you how to put them to sleep?'

'You're having me on. How can you put a yabby to sleep?'

Thomas reached in gingerly and plucked out a writhing yabby. He found a flat rock nearby, and sat the yabby upside-down on its head. Then with his index finger, he rubbed its coiled back. After only a few seconds, he moved his hand away and the yabby remained in a comatose state, still on its head on the rock.

'You can leave them like that for ages,' he said, getting up and going to the knapsack where he produced a billycan and a box of matches.

Mikaela looked at the yabby, amazed that it hadn't moved.

'That has to be the weirdest piece of animal behaviour I have ever seen.'

'You've lived with me for a few months. That's got to be pretty weird.'

She watched him as he cleared a space and found some leaves and twigs. In a short time he had a fire going. He filled the billy with dam water and sat it on the fire.

'Once it's boiling we'll throw them in.'

'Poor things,' Mikaela repeated. ' I know, maybe we could put them all to sleep before we put them into the water.'

Thomas gave her a sideways look.

'I've never seen that done before. But go ahead.'

Mikaela found a number of flat rocks and started to pull out the yabbies, one by one, and copy Thomas' actions. By the tenth yabby she had got it down to a fine art. But by this time the water was boiling.

'It's time, Mikaela girl.'

She stood up, rubbing her stiff back from where she had been leaning over. The yabbies made a very strange sight, lined up next to each other on rocks, all motionless and up-side-down.

'But I've only done ten.'

'Never mind, you've made a difference for at least half of our lunch. Let's put them in.'

They dropped the yabbies into the water, and the ones from the bucket that had settled anyway in the warmth of the sun. Thomas stirred the billy with a stick then settled back onto the ground. Mikaela sat beside him, and looked over the dam. Insects were whirring across the surface of the water.

'They won't take long. Now, how about you start from the beginning…'

Mikaela took a deep breath. They had had such a lovely morning – in a way it seemed a pity to dredge up the events of the past few weeks. But that was the reason they were here, and because the day was perfect, it had paved the way for meaningful conversation.

'The beginning…' Mikaela murmured. What was the beginning? Was it when Bill had died, or was it before that, when they had come home from Tasmania and Thomas had been so busy?

Mikaela began to explain her feelings over the last months, talking things over to explain them to herself as much as to Thomas. She had struggled being the new wife of a farmer, struggled with the loneliness and the responsibility and the different life that it was. She had felt deserted as Thomas had gone to work each morning, and even though she had her work at the school, she would still come home to a large empty house in the middle of nowhere. She had enjoyed Bill's company, but she still blamed herself in part for his death. She had never encouraged Zac to show her attention, but he had crept his way into her life and for some reason he was there when she needed comfort. She had no excuses, but she had explanations.

Thomas listened in silence while she spoke, nodding occasionally. After a while she stopped speaking and he got up to pick the billycan off the fire. He drained the water out over the flames, then tipped the cooked yabbies into the bucket.

'Careful, they're hot.'

They spent a few moments picking and peeling shells, and chewing on the tasty flesh. The yabby flavour was strong and pungent, much stronger than the flavour of prawns from the supermarket. Mikaela enjoyed the taste, and for a while they were content to sit and eat. After a moment, Thomas spoke.

'Mikaela, it's hard to listen to some of what you're saying, and it's going to take me a while to understand about you and Zac, but I don't want you to feel guilty anymore about any of it. Like I said yesterday, I was too wrapped up in my own problems to see that you were having a hard time. Will you forgive me for that?'

Mikaela nodded and felt tears begin to well up in her eyes.

'Of course I'll forgive you, Thomas, but there's really nothing to forgive. What I did, on the other hand, was stupid. I'm not sure if you'll ever be able to forgive me.'

'I forgive you, Mikaela, a hundred times over. I've prayed about it, and God showed me a long time ago that we should never live without forgiving. It creates bitterness, and I've been there before.'

The tears rolled over Mikaela's eyes and spilled onto her cheeks. The weeks of enduring sadness and emotional up-heaval finally began to melt away. Thomas moved closer to her and hugged her tightly and she allowed herself to weep openly in his arms.

'Can we start again, Thomas? From this day, can we start all over?'

'We can start all over every day, Mikaela. I think that's what's so great about God. We can leave all the rubbish with him and he can get rid of it and make us clean. Just trust Him, Mikaela.'

They held each other for a long time, Mikaela feeling peace at last in her husband's arms.

After a while, she pulled away, wiping her eyes with her hand, the smell of yabbies strong on her skin.

'I must look awful,' she smiled.

'I don't care,' Thomas replied, grinning.

'I just remembered something about Zac, something he

told me when he was really angry that day.'

'We need to get the police onto Zac. He needs to be locked up.'

'I don't think it would do any good, Thomas. Bonnie won't talk.'

'Hmm, we'll see. What were you going to tell me?'

'Zac said that you had bullied him at school, that you had buried him in some hole underground and put a piece of tin over the top.'

Thomas's face looked blank.

'What? I don't remember that. Why would I do that?'

Mikaela shrugged.

'It didn't sound like you. Apparently the day it happened was the day his father killed himself. He didn't get to see his father because he was stuck in the hole.'

Thomas shook his head.

'That's a very sad story, but I think Zac must be getting me confused with someone else.'

'Well, he's holding you responsible, Thomas. You may need to watch your back.'

'He might spray me from the plane, you mean? I think I saw a movie about that once.' Thomas was grinning.

'Don't joke, Thomas. I really think Zac's capable of anything. You can tell when you look into his eyes.'

'I don't want to hear anything about you looking into his eyes,' Thomas said, giving her a gentle push on the arm.

'I don't mean in that way…'

'Then let's forget about it.'

'But Thomas…'

'We're starting again, remember? Let's put it out of our minds and get back to life, the way it should have been from the beginning.'

He tossed his remaining yabby shells into the dam and reached over to take Mikaela's hand and pull her towards him.

'It feels like we haven't been together for so long,' he breathed into her ear.

'Thomas, we're in a paddock.'

'I know, but there's no-one around.'

'And you smell like a big yabby.'

Thomas hesitated for a moment then screwed up his nose.

'You're right. We both smell like dead fish. I'll take you home and we'll get cleaned up.'

They tidied the area beside the dam and re-hung the net and bucket in the Mallee trees. Then Thomas started up the bike and together they sped over the green paddocks, back towards the place Mikaela now felt she could truly call home.

Chapter Seventeen

The next few weeks were blissful. Mikaela woke each morning looking forward to the day ahead. Small things that she had never noticed before suddenly became special – the sun making patterns on the wall through the lace of the bedroom curtains, the comforting clucking of the hens that she could hear from the orchard, the smell of hot coffee on a cold morning. She enjoyed her work at the school, and equally enjoyed coming home and preparing a tasty meal to share with Thomas. It was like falling in love all over again.

The school holidays arrived and Thomas and Mikaela spent quality time together, working on the house and the garden, and discussing ideas for the future of the farm. Mikaela felt that they were functioning as a team, rather than separate entities with entirely different lives. It was a good feeling.

Together they also decided that they would rejoin the youth group leadership team. They had always enjoyed working with the youth, and although David and Andy had said they could have as much time off as they wanted, it had been part of their relationship-building before they had married, and it would be good to continue in an outreach away from the farm.

Youth group was held on Friday nights, usually at the hall beside the church. As Mikaela and Thomas opened the door of the hall on this particular Friday, she took his hand and held it tightly. This was their first youth group meeting as a married couple. It felt good to have Thomas by her side, and to know that he was hers.

The young people inside gave a cheer as the two entered. The hall was lit fully and the heaters were on, giving it a warm friendly atmosphere. David came over to shake Thomas' hand, his face beaming.

'Great to have you both back on board.' He beckoned them in to the crowd and for a while they mingled, greeting young people they had not seen since earlier in the year. After a moment, David called the group together.

'Welcome everyone. Tonight we extend a special welcome to Mr and Mrs McDowell…'

A cheer went up from the gathered youth and a few wolf whistles were sounded. Thomas inclined his head in acknowledgement, his hand holding fast to Mikaela's.

'Because of the wonderful return of our esteemed leaders, tonight we have decided to give them a treat. We are going to create for them a delicious dessert – banana split with chocolate topping.' A sigh of approval went up from the crowd. 'But - there will be something special about this banana split. It will be the longest banana split ever made in the Mallee.'

On cue, Andy wheeled himself in from the kitchen area. He was holding one end of a piece of PVC pipe that had been sawn in half lengthways. Following him were two more members of the youth group, who were holding the remaining length of the pipe. By the time the three of them had entered the hallway and Andy had reached the front door, the pipe extended the length of the hall. They placed it down on the floor.

'Time for the bananas!' David called out, and then everyone was diving into the cardboard boxes that were placed at the sides of the hall, pulling out bananas and peeling them. Someone was in charge of the knife and the bananas were sliced up and placed into the pipe until it was full of banana from one end to the other.

'Ice cream!' Emily emerged from the kitchen with a large tub of ice cream, which was then passed between hands. The members of the youth group each knelt beside the pipe and spooned liberal amounts of ice cream on top of the banana. Next David was handing around bottles of chocolate topping and a jar of hundreds and thousands. The place was a frenzy of laughter and sweet-smelling food. Hundreds and thousands were sprayed all over the place and quite a few large pools of topping were forming on the floor.

'And now...' said David. The hall hushed and the students stepped back from their glorious creation. 'Now...our guests of honour must have the first taste.'

Mikaela looked at Thomas and giggled nervously.

'Okay...' she said hesitantly.

'But wait, there's a catch.'

'I knew there would be,' Thomas muttered.

'Thomas must feed Mikaela, and Mikaela must feed Thomas – and you both must be blind folded.'

The crowd screamed in delight. Before she knew what was happening, Mikaela felt someone's hands near her face and a tea towel was pulled tightly around her eyes. She continued to clutch Thomas' hand, laughing out loud, and together they stumbled towards the pipe of dessert. Thomas must have felt it with his foot, because he pulled her down beside him and she reached forward and touched the pipe.

'Could we have a spoon?' Thomas' voice came from beside her left ear.

'A spoon? Oh dear,' David's voice was mocking pity. 'I'm afraid we accidentally dropped the spoon…underneath one of the bananas!'

The crowd cheered again, and a chant began.

'Spoon! Spoon!'

Mikaela could feel her laughter becoming uncontrollable. She thrust her hand into the cold ice cream and banana mess and dug around for the spoon.

'I think we might have to give up on the spoon,' she heard Thomas say.

'Just use your hands then,' Andy's voice sounded from somewhere in the room.

'Okay,' agreed Mikaela. 'Here you are, darling.' She scooped up whatever mess she could feel and held it out in the direction of her husband's face. The crowd went wild, laughing and cheering.

'Thank-you, dearest. You just put it all over my head.'

'Oh sorry, let me try again.' This time she felt there was some success as she pushed the muck into Thomas' mouth.

'Your turn,' he spluttered, and in the next moment there was a cold gooey feeling over her cheeks and the room exploded in laughter.

'We must look ridiculous,' Mikaela chuckled.

'You've hit the nail on the head,' David said. 'And we've got a camera here, so you'll get a good look at yourselves.'

The couple were eventually allowed to take off their tea towels to survey the amount of food they were wearing, and then the whole group tucked in to the enormous banana split – with spoons. Mikaela and Thomas ate with them, laughing and chatting, until finally the kettle was put on and everyone lined up for Milo and tea. Mikaela fished out a sponge from the sink, and took it back out into the hall, wiping at her shirt.

'You'll just have to take the whole thing off,' Andy said, coming up beside her.

'In your dreams,' Mikaela smiled. She sat down beside her cousin.

'Did I happen to mention I was going down to Melbourne next weekend?' Andy continued in a casual manner.

'No,' Mikaela replied, hearing something curious in his voice.

'I have a date.'

'You do? In Melbourne? That's a bit of a distance for a date.'

'You're just surprised I have a date at all, Mikaela, be it Melbourne or anywhere.'

'Don't put words into my mouth, Andy. I'm not surprised you have a date at all.'

He raised his eyebrows and waited for a moment.

'Not really…' she continued, feeling embarrassed.

'I'll forgive you this once for not being honest, Mikaela. Don't forget, this is Andy you're talking to. I can see right through women.'

'Please, spare me. So am I allowed to ask who the lucky lady is and how on earth you met?'

'We met at your wedding.'

This time Mikaela could feel genuine surprise across her face.

'You don't mean-'

'Erin. I haven't had a chance to tell you that we've been emailing quite a lot since you kids got married.'

'I had no idea. Erin keeps things pretty close to her heart.'

'She doesn't blab, you mean. I think that's why I like her. She's honest and she's not too sugary.'

175

'Strange, I thought you liked sugary.'

'Maybe I've changed. Anyway, she's invited me to spend the weekend at her parent's house. I'm looking forward to it.'

'I'm really happy for you, Andy. Erin's a great girl. And you're right, she's honest. I just hope she doesn't say anything too blunt.'

'I'm a big boy, I'll cope.' He gave Mikaela a smile, and then glanced at Thomas who was across the room. 'So, how are things with you two? You both look pretty happy. You told him, then?'

Mikaela nodded.

'Of course. You were right, it was ridiculous to think I could exist with a secret like that on my heart. We're great now. It's like turning over a new leaf.'

'That's good to see. I knew you'd figure it out. You're good at that, Mikaela. You get your strength from God.'

'I nearly didn't this time. I nearly gave Him away all together.'

Andy shook his head.

'No you didn't. God's got his hand firmly around your heart, Mikaela McDowell. He wouldn't have let you get too far down the road of life by yourself.'

Mikaela looked at Andy and just felt love for him. She reached across and gave him a quick hug.

'You're a great guy, Andy. I am privileged to be related to you.'

'Is this a private party?' Emily pulled up a chair and placed three cups of hot Milo on the table beside them. 'Have you got yourself cleaned up then?'

'No. I hope you guys are insured for chocolate stains.'

'We're probably not insured for anything,' commented Andy dryly.

Emily passed her a steaming mug.

'Mikaela, I wanted to ask you whether you had anything planned for Thomas' thirtieth?'

Mikaela hesitated. Thomas' birthday was in early September – that was just over a month away. She knew that he would be turning thirty, and had assumed she would have a meal at home with the family and a few friends. Apart from that, she had no other 'plans'.

'The only reason I ask,' continued Emily, 'is that Mum and I were talking the other day, and we thought we should help you out. After all, we couldn't expect you to go to all the trouble of hiring the town hall and organising the catering.'

'The town hall? Catering? I thought we'd just have tea at home.'

Emily shook her head.

'I know, that's the easiest, and that's what I would want to do. But in Turramore, you've got to celebrate your thirtieth in a big way, especially if you're a footballer. Everyone wants to come and give the birthday lad their best wishes.'

'Okay…' Mikaela hesitated, trying to get the idea around her head, 'so in that case, we are going to need to start getting organised soon. Like now.'

Emily nodded and laughed.

'Mikaela, you should see yourself. You've gone as white as the ice cream in your hair. Don't let it worry you, we'll all pitch in and help. That's what we're here for. Mum has friends who can provide food and I can organise the hall. David can get hold of a band – and there you have it.'

'It sounds a bit too easy.'

'It is. You'll have the tricky part – figuring out who to invite!'

Andy shook his head as he sipped from his Milo.

'Good luck, Mik. You can deal with that dilemma on your own.'

*****

When they returned home that evening, Mikaela sat down at the kitchen table with a notebook and pen, and began listing details about Thomas' party. On a separate page she noted down names of people she would invite. She discovered happily that she was quite excited about organising a party for her husband. It was something she could do to show him how much she loved him, how much she appreciated his forgiveness and his strength of character.

Thomas poked his head from around the hallway corner.

'What are you doing at this hour?'

'Organising your thirtieth birthday party.'

'I thought we were just having a roast.'

'Not now. We're going to have a full-on shindig, and it's going to be in the town hall.'

Thomas rolled his eyes.

'A full-on shindig - let me guess, was this my little sister's idea?'

'Yes, and your mum's, and I think it's a good one. People around this town really appreciate you, Thomas, and this way they'll be able to show you how they feel.'

'Sounds a bit mushy.'

'It'll be great. You'll have to make a list of who you want to invite and what sort of food you'd like.'

'Well, I know one thing we won't be having – banana split. I'll be happy if we don't see another banana for the rest of the year.'

'I'll make a note of that, Mr McDowell.'

'And as far as guests go…there's really only one guest I want there.'

Mikaela raised her eyebrows and smiled as Thomas came nearer.

'And who would that be?'

'I think you know.' And he reached to take her hand and

lead her out of the kitchen.

Chapter Eighteen

For the next few weeks, Mikaela was wonderfully pre-occupied with the organisation of Thomas' party. It took up most of her conversation, and she wondered whether Thomas was getting tired of questions like 'what's you favourite colour', and 'where can I find some of your old football photos', and 'would you prefer fruitcake or mud-cake'. He simply smiled and answered as best he could, and she wondered whether he realised that this was part of the healing process for Mikaela, and something she wanted to do especially for him as a form of thanks.

A few evenings before the big day, she sat out on the front porch, watching the sky change from pink to orange as the sunset. Two weeks ago she would not have been able to sit outside at this time – it would have been too cold. Now the weather was changing and the chill that had once brought a biting cold to the air had vanished, leaving behind a fresh breeze. She could see that buds were starting to form on the plum trees at the side of the house, and when she had fed the chickens that morning she had noticed that the whole orchard was starting to bud. It was like new life springing up every-where, a new beginning starting all over the farm.

She had read some of her Bible, and now she picked up the diary she had brought out with her, and flicked through the pages. It had been so interesting reading about farm life back when Carolyn had been in Turramore. Some things had changed a great deal, but other things appeared to be just the same. She had read so many of the entries. Now she skipped across to the final one.

October 30th, 1977
It looks like I will have to leave. Gareth will not accept me as I am, will not accept this baby we have made together. I have loved Gareth with my whole heart and yet he has put up walls between us. I know abortion is wrong, and yet what can I do? I am so lost, so confused. Maybe there is another way. Maybe I can talk to Billy, dearest darling Billy, who loves me and marshmallows and the copper house.

The entry finished, and although there were a few pages remaining in the diary, they were blank. Mikaela closed the book and shivered. Gareth had once told her that he had never found the courage to read the diary himself. Maybe if he had he would have understood Carolyn's fear of abortion. He would have wondered about Billy, and he may have even guessed that she didn't go through with the abortion after all. But Gareth's mind had been in no state to absorb Carolyn's writings, even if he had decided to look into the pages.

Mikaela wondered if Carolyn had in fact spoken to Bill of her troubles. Perhaps she had told him that she was going to have the baby. Maybe he had remembered that somehow and knew of Mikaela's existence before Elizabeth had even told him. But then maybe in his mind he was expecting Mikaela to still be a baby. And he had called her Lynny so many times, it was difficult to know how much he understood.

Bill's words came back to her as she sat on the porch, the temperature beginning to drop. Bill put it in the copper house. Bill hide it for you. She realised there was only one other person whom she could ask about the copper house, and that was Elizabeth.

On Saturday she was to meet her aunt at the town hall to decorate the place before the party. That would be her opportunity to ask about Bill and his house of copper.

*****

The sparrows were chirping outside when Mikaela woke Thomas with a kiss.

'Happy birthday, love of my life.' She handed him a small package wrapped in gold paper.

'I thought you liked to sleep in on Saturdays,' he mumbled, rubbing his eyes. Mikaela liked the way he looked in the mornings, all crumpled and creased, like a rag-doll. She kissed him again and watched him open the present. He pulled the gold fob watch from the box, his eyes wide.

'Mikaela, this is too much.'

'It was my grandfather's. Dad gave it to me years ago, and I decided I would give it to my husband.'

'It's probably worth a fortune. I'd be afraid to use it.'

'It doesn't matter. It's yours now. Grandpa would have approved.'

'Thank you, Mikaela.' They embraced for a moment, and then Mikaela jumped out of bed.

'Today's going to be busy. I've got to get things ready down at the hall, check on the food…'

'This is like another wedding.'

Mikaela changed into an old pair of jeans and a worn green sweatshirt, talking as she pulled on the clothes.

'I'm going to make you bacon and eggs for breakfast, then I want you to relax here at home, have a nice long shower, all that sort of thing. I'm doing all the work today, and you just have a rest.'

'What if I get bored?'

'Then go and feed the chooks. But I don't want to see you at the hall, because the decorations and everything are a surprise.'

'You're the boss…'

'I am today.'

In a few moments she had bacon sizzling in the pan and was cracking some eggs. The kettle had boiled and she made a cup of tea. Thomas wandered into the kitchen and she sat him down in front of the steaming breakfast, kissing the top of his head.

'Enjoy your breakfast, and I'll be back a bit later to check up on you.'

He shook his head, grinning, and she left him in the kitchen.

The morning was fresh and crisp. It was going to be a perfect day. The crops around her as she drove into town were beautiful, high and green and lush. There was no football today, as the team had a bye. It was just one more piece of the plan that had worked out perfectly. It meant that Thomas' football team could come to the party, which was due to start in the afternoon.

The town hall was already unlocked when she arrived. Memories of her wedding came back to her as she wandered into the echoing building, her feet resounding on the wooden floor, the stage at the end where the band had played. A different band would be playing this evening, more of a rock and roll feel. The old place must have heard such an assortment of music in its history.

She found Elizabeth already in the kitchen, sorting through

scissors and streamers. Behind her were white ceramic pots with dark blue balloons on sticks poking up from each one.

'Good morning, honey. These were on the front step when I arrived, so I just brought them in here.'

'They look great. I ordered them last week.'

'And what about these streamers – are they okay? They were the only ones I could find in Leighton.'

'They look fine, Elizabeth. Let's hang them up.'

They started straight away with the decorations, and it took them over an hour before they were satisfied with the effect. Together they shifted out trestle tables and set them up around the hall, putting cloths over them and the balloons on each table. After another hour, it was time for a break.

'I can't believe it's almost lunch time,' puffed Mikaela, as they put the kettle on in the kitchen area. 'Helen and Emily will be here soon to organise the food.'

'The place looks really nice, Mikaela. I think you have a flair for decorating.'

'It's pretty easy when you just go for blue, blue and blue. Thomas didn't seem particularly creative when I asked him to suggest a colour scheme.'

They sat on chairs for a moment in the hall, sipping on their tea.

'Oh, I almost forgot,' Elizabeth said, putting her tea-cup down on the floor. She reached into the pocket of her shirt and pulled out a square of tissue. 'We were talking at Bill's funeral about Carolyn's things. I wanted to give you this.'

Mikaela opened the tissue and pulled out a necklace. It was a simple silver pendant, somewhat darkened with age, with a round black stone in the centre and hanging from a silver chain.

'Carolyn made it – the pendant, that is. The chain was just a cheap one she picked up from somewhere. She started to do a bit of jewellery making, and this was one of her first pieces. She wore it a lot.'

Mikaela fingered the pendant slowly.

'Thank you, Elizabeth, but I'm not sure I can take it. It was left for you.'

'Well, it wasn't really left for anyone. She wasn't meant to die so soon. So you are entitled to it as much as I am – more so, probably.'

Mikaela opened the clasp and attached the necklace around her neck.

'Do you think I can wear it? Is that…okay?'

'I think it looks fine on you.'

'I mean…'

'I know what you mean, dear, and I still think it's fine.'

Mikaela touched the necklace and was silent for a moment. Elizabeth's reference to the funeral reminded her of her question.

'Before I forget, Elizabeth, I've been meaning to ask you about something that Bill kept telling me about. A copper house. He mentioned it a few times, and it's in Carolyn's diary. Do you know what a copper house is?'

Elizabeth gazed up to the ceiling, her eyes concentrating hard.

'Copper house…no, I don't think I know what that is. You say Bill talked about it?'

Mikaela sat slumped in her chair, her last hope of discovering the meaning of the words fading.

'Yes. He talked about a fire being in the copper house, and how it was very warm. That's about all he said.'

Elizabeth's face suddenly brightened as realisation rushed across her features.

'Oh, he must have meant the old shed with the copper in it.'

'The copper?'

'Way back when we were young, my grandmother and her

sister used to make milk coffee for the social dances that were held out at the hall on the Turramore east road. They used to heat water up in a huge round tub made of copper, then sit a big can of milk into the water to warm the milk up.'

'And all this took place inside a house?'

Elizabeth shook her head.

'No, it was in a little old tin shed behind the hall. The copper sat in a cast iron frame on top of a fire. I remember now that Bill used to sit in the shed on the winter nights when there were dances in the hall. He would sit there where it was warm and watch my grandmother making the coffee for the people at the dance. He must have been very young.'

'He still remembered it.'

'That's quite amazing, isn't it? I guess back then the shed must have been a bit like a house to a tiny boy. A 'copper house'.'

She retrieved her cup and sipped at it, while Mikaela just sat thinking. The answer hadn't been what she was expecting, but what had she been expecting?

'I guess it's gone now, the shed.'

'No, I think it's still there. It hasn't been used for years and years, and I think it's pretty much falling down, but it's still there as far as I know.'

'Out near Carolyn's hall somewhere?'

'Straight out the back.'

Mikaela nodded to herself, then heard noise at the doorway. Emily and her mother were coming into the hall, laden with trays and serving implements. Elizabeth and Mikaela went over to help them bring the items into the kitchen.

'We've got another load in the car,' Emily panted, going back outside.

'The caterers will be here in another hour or so to set up,' Helen explained. 'We just have to make sure the kitchen's clean and ready, and that we have enough cutlery and crockery.'

'Thanks for doing all this,' Mikaela said, giving her mother-in-law a hug.

'I enjoy it, dear. Thomas is a wonderful son and he has married a wonderful wife. I would do anything for you two.'

Her words made Mikaela's face flush. Helen still thought she was wonderful. Maybe one day Mikaela would be able to accept the complement, but not just yet.

The women busied themselves with the kitchen, and finished off details in the hall, and then Elizabeth left to go up the street and buy some sausage rolls for dinner. The time marched on.

Mikaela was sweeping up the last of the dust from the floor when she noticed the louvered glass panels that ran along the tops of the walls on each side. There were cobwebs dangling from the corners and the glass looked quite dirty.

'What do you think about the windows up there, Emily? They're pretty bad.'

Emily peered at the louvres.

'I don't know, Mikaela. That's a big job, cleaning them at this stage. How about we just give them a dust off and get rid of the Daddy-Long-Legs?'

They found a long handled brush that Emily began to use on one side of the hall. On the other, Mikaela set up a small ladder that had been sitting at the back of the stage area, and began to run a cloth along the glass. It was annoying and dirty work, but it would certainly make the hall look brighter.

Mikaela began to open up the louvres as she went, to sweep the spiders and insects outside. She was almost half way along the row, when she noticed someone through the opened glass. A man was walking on the other side of the road, across from the hall, a shopping bag in his hand. He was wearing overalls and a hat, and was moving quickly, his head down. She watched him while she kept cleaning, noticing a twitch that was apparent in his left shoulder. He paused before he crossed the road and pulled something from his pocket, checking it quickly then replacing it. He then crossed the road and walked over to a ute which was parked in front of the café.

Mikaela felt her hands and knees go weak as two revelations came to her instantaneously. The object the man had removed from his pocket was a gun and the ute he had climbed into was a sickly yellow colour. The vehicle started up then lurched away down the road.

Zac Hamilton was back in Turramore.

Mikaela turned and watched Emily on the other side of the hall, still cleaning. Elizabeth had returned with the sausage rolls and she and Helen were rattling around in the kitchen area. Everyone was totally oblivious to what Mikaela had just seen and the feelings of dread that were rising in her.

She paused to think for a moment. Zac was in town, but that didn't necessarily mean anything. He could just be shopping for his aunt. On the other hand, he had a gun with him, hidden in his pocket. The sight of guns made Mikaela wary at the best of times. Now Zac, who had looked rather nervous and twitchy, had a gun and had driven away at top speed. There was a foreboding in her bones that she could not explain. He could be heading back home to Mrs Hamilton, dear poor Mrs Hamilton who wouldn't know what was happening if he pulled the gun on her. Or he could be heading to McDowell Hill to find Mikaela. She rubbed her wrist as she remembered his words. I'll come back…we'll go away together, just you and I…

Only he wouldn't find Mikaela at McDowell Hill. He would only find Thomas, Thomas who was probably having a sleep in front of the television or sitting unsuspecting out in the orchard…

She jumped down from the ladder, tipping it over with a crash that resounded through the hall.

'Mikaela, are you alright?' Emily called.

'I need a phone – is there a phone around here?'

'I've got the mobile, but there's no coverage here in Turramore. There's a phone box outside the café.'

'Okay, come with me.'

She ran outside into the sunshine and across the road, vaguely aware of Emily following her. The day that had been so beautiful to her now seemed dull and uninteresting. She could no longer appreciate it – its beauty was for other folk. She reached the box and yanked the phone from its cradle. She had change in her pocket that she had been keeping to buy something to eat, and she threw the coins into the machine, dialling the number with shaking fingers.

The phone at McDowell Hill was ringing. She listened to the tone repeating over and over in the handset.

'Pick up the phone,' she whispered, closing her eyes. She heard Emily open the phone box door behind her. Suddenly there was a click, and Thomas' voice came on the line.

'McDowell residence.'

'Thomas! It's me. I just saw Zac in the street. I don't know where he's heading but I wanted to warn you. He's got a gun.'

Behind her she heard Emily breathe in sharply. There was a moment's silence on the end of the phone.

'Alright,' said Thomas, his voice calm. 'I'll keep my eyes open. Are you almost finished with the hall?'

'Yes.'

'Maybe you should go home with Mum or Em. I'll call you there once I know things are safe.'

'What about Mrs Hamilton? I'm worried about her too.'

She waited for a moment. There was no answer.

'Thomas?'

'Hang on…someone's turning into the drive…' There was a click, and suddenly the line was disconnected, leaving Mikaela with an eerie beeping sound.

'Thomas!' she yelled into the phone, knowing there was no way he could hear her.

'What's going on?' Emily asked, her face white.

'It's Zac Hamilton. He's at the homestead. You need to call the police, Emily, and tell them to get out to McDowell Hill as quickly as possible. Get onto David too, anyone you can think of.'

'What are you going to do?'

'I'm going to drive out there. Maybe I can talk to him.'

'Don't be ridiculous, Mikaela. Let the police deal with it.'

'There may not be time. The police could be on a call anywhere in the district.'

She squeezed Emily's arm and ran back up the road to the hall where she had left her ute. In a moment she had started the engine, and wheeled the machine out onto the road that headed west.

Chapter Nineteen

The palms of her hands were so wet with perspiration that a number of times they slipped on the steering wheel and she almost careened into the fence line. Her heart was racing and her breath was coming out in little gasps. The road was so long, it was longer today than it had ever been before. Mile after mile seemed to go past, green paddocks, more green paddocks – it was endless.

They hadn't thought about Zac for months. They had forgotten all about him, never mentioning his name, and purposefully putting him out of their minds. It had been wonderful not to have his presence hanging over their lives. But Zac had obviously not forgotten anything.

'Be with Thomas, be with Thomas,' she prayed through parched lips, her eyes wide and straining ahead for any sign of movement on the road. Maybe Zac had spoken with Thomas and she would see his ute leave to go up to his aunt's. Maybe it hadn't been his ute arriving at McDowell Hill at all. Maybe…maybe…

McDowell Hill came into view. She hooked the ute so sharply to the right that the back wheels spun in the gravel and she was forced to take the vehicle over a grassy embankment before getting back onto the driveway. A sick feeling rose in her as she saw the yellow ute parked by the front fence. She pulled her own vehicle to a stop and jumped out, running around to the back of the house.

'Thomas!' she yelled, but came to a halt when she reached the back porch. Smeared across the pale verandah floor at the back door was blood. There was a shoeprint, a handprint, a long slash of the scarlet mess running down across the floor towards the laundry block. Mikaela put a hand out to the wall to steady herself, afraid she was either going to be sick or faint, thereby becoming useless to help anybody. She looked away from the bloody scene, and as she did she caught sight of movement in the doorway of the gardening storeroom. Zac was there, leaning against the doorjamb, watching her. Blood was streaked across his face and over the front of his overalls. From his bloody hands dangled the key to the cellar.

He was smiling at her, a face that at any other time would have been considered handsome, but was now macabre in its enjoyment.

'It's good to see you again, Mikaela. I've missed you.'

The voice was quiet, but slightly out of breath.

'Where's Thomas? What have you done?'

'Thomas has gone, Mikaela. It's just you and me now, like it was always meant to be.'

'You don't know what you're talking about.'

'Yes I do, Mikaela. Thomas had everything – I had nothing. I've changed all that now.' His left shoulder gave a sudden violent twitch, but he didn't seem to notice.

'Zac, you're not well,' Mikaela said, trying to bring her voice down to sound more calm. 'I can take you somewhere

where people can help you.'

'I'm not seeing any shrink, Mikaela. They tried to get Dad to see a shrink, but he knew there was nothing wrong with his brain. He was clever, my Dad, but not clever enough to see the train coming.'

'I thought he took his own life.'

Zac hesitated for a moment, then his eyes narrowed.

'My father would never do that. He would never leave me on purpose.'

Mikaela took a deep breath to steady her voice and her emotions. She could see the blood on the porch from the corner of her eye.

'Zac, you've been through a lot. But there are others who've experienced the same sorts of things. There is help out there, I don't mean shrinks, I just mean...help.' She slowly put out her hand, but was aware of it shaking. 'Why don't you let me help you?'

Zac smiled and shook his head.

'I know what you're trying to do, dear sweet Mikaela. It's not going to work. Nothing is going to work except us.'

Before she knew what was happening, he had taken two large steps towards her and had grabbed her wrists, wrenching her arms behind her. She gasped with the pain, but then he was pushing her roughly towards the front gate. She tried to struggle, but he pulled her arms back even further until she thought she would collapse. They reached the gate, but just as they opened it, another vehicle turned off of the main road. It was a white van, and it drove down the driveway slowly and pulled to a stop beside the other utilities, its engine spluttering slightly. Out stepped a large bearded figure wearing an old t-shirt and faded jeans.

'G'day, Mrs McDowell. I got that order of cheese that you wanted.' Joey Boland grinned at her from under his cap as he opened up the back of his van.

Mikaela felt Zac's grip on her relax slightly, and she wondered for a moment if she might be able to run. But in the next second something hard and metallic was pushed into her skin through her jumper, and she knew that Zac had the gun held to her back.

'Thanks Joey, but I'm not sure if I'll be needing it today after all.'

'But isn't it for Thomas' party?' He looked up at her from where he had been fossicking in the van, and suddenly seemed to notice Zac.

'Maybe it would be best if you took it into the hall yourself. It might stay colder.'

Joey said nothing but kept his eyes fixed on Zac.

'I don't think I know you. I'm Joey Boland, the fishman.'

'Zac. I'm a friend of the family.'

'Are you okay, mate? Is that blood on you?'

Mikaela wanted to scream out to Joey for help, but the gun in her back kept her mind focussed. Joey was now in danger too.

'Zac's been cutting up a sheep for us,' she managed to say, struggling to keep her voice steady.

'Oh, okay,' Joey nodded. He still hadn't smiled at Zac, and Mikaela could see suspicion in his face. 'Well, I'd better get going then, and I'll get this cheese into town.'

'Thanks Joey. Oh, and by the way…'

Joey hesitated as he went around to the door of the van.
'Yes?'

'You remember that fertilizer that Thomas ordered - I'd like to order another bag. Could you do that for me?'

Joey looked at her strangely for a moment, and Mikaela wondered if Zac was getting restless with the charade they were playing. But then he nodded.

'Sure thing, Mrs McDowell.' He got back into the van,

and then headed slowly back up the driveway and out onto the road towards town.

Immediately Zac pushed her towards his ute, opening the driver door and hoisting her up. He followed her into the cabin, the gun trained on her the whole time. Starting the engine, he threw the vehicle into gear, and sped up the driveway.

'You're a clever girl, Mikaela. I thought I was going to have to keep that one quiet – permanently.'

Mikaela said nothing. The whole scene with Joey had taken its toll on her emotional state of mind. She was feeling numb, the reality of what was happening beginning to sink in. She still had no idea what had happened to Thomas. He could be lying wounded in the house, or hiding waiting for help. She refused to even consider the notion that he was dead. If she began to think about that possibility, she knew she would lose all control. As it was, she wasn't going to be able to stay in control for very much longer.

Zac continued to talk, and as he did she heard his voice become softer.

'I'm going to put the gun away now, Mikaela. I hated to use it like that. I know it scared you. There's no point in trying to get away, because I'll just get it out again and then I'll have to use it properly. So let's pretend none of that ever happened, hey?'

He flashed a smile at her from behind the wheel. She felt like slapping him in the face, but instead she turned her head and looked out of the window. They were heading west, and it wasn't long before she saw the Hamilton cottage.

Zac pulled the ute into the gates and drove up around the side of the house to the backyard. He pulled to a halt with a jerk, and got out, yanking Mikaela out with him. The yard seemed messier than ever, with junk and rubbish strewn everywhere. Mikaela tried to see into the kitchen window as Zac pulled her along.

'Where's you aunt?'

'Aunty got in the way.'

Mikaela swallowed the bile that had suddenly risen in her throat.

The chickens must have escaped from their pen and were now squawking and pecking around the yard, lost and forlorn. An old windmill squeaked eerily from the other side of the house. Zac led her around a group of gum trees further down the yard.

The plane stood there waiting, its shiny red and white paintwork glinting in the afternoon sun. Mikaela stared at it. It was like a nightmare coming true, and there was no way to wake up.

'Right, it's time for our little flight.'

'Where are you taking me?'

'As far away as possible. They won't find us. We'll go inland, I think, and get lost among the sand dunes. We'll have a lot of time to get to know each other.'

'But Zac, you told me this plane only has one seat.'

'It does. But it also has the spray bin.'

He smiled at her, as if she would completely understand and accept what he was saying.

'You'll be safe enough. And I'll be able to concentrate on flying. It will work well for us both.'

'You must be joking. I'm not getting into a spray bin.'

'You will, Mikaela, because there's no other way.'

In a moment of panic she jerked away from him, and might have succeeded in running except that her shoe caught on a tree root and she fell to the ground. Before she could get up, he was on top of her, pinning her to the earth. His knee was in her back and one hand pushed her face into the dirt.

'Don't run, Mikaela, it just annoys me and it wastes time.' He was whispering fiercely into her ear, his voice thin and hard. She closed her eyes to escape the terror of his face and felt the tears of total fear begin to seep from her eyes. Panic was finally starting to set in.

Then suddenly there was another voice.

'Get off her.' She felt Zac's body go rigid, and opening one eye she could see a man beside the house, silhouetted against the sky, a shot-gun raised to his shoulder and pointing straight towards them.

'Do it, or I'll blow your head off.' She felt Zac shift his weight from her, and suddenly she found it easier to breathe.

The man's voice was raspy and hard, but very familiar. Raising her head she saw Thomas. He didn't look at her - his eyes were trained down the barrel of the gun, never moving it from its target. His clothes were dirty and covered in dark muck, and his skin was pale and shone with sweat, but he remained absolutely still. Appearing from the other side of the house was Joey, also armed with a rifle.

'I thought you were dead, Thomas,' she heard Zac say. She moved slowly to one side and pulled herself up, leaning against a tree as she did. Zac saw her move but did nothing to prevent it – the rifle remained trained on him.

'The police are on their way, Zac,' Thomas said quietly. 'What are you going to do?'

For a moment Zac hesitated. His hand moved slightly towards the pocket of his overalls, where Mikaela knew he had hidden his gun.

'Don't move them hands or we'll blow them off too.' Joey's voice carried loudly across the yard.

Zac stopped moving his hand and stood frozen. His eyes flicked around him like a scared dog, and Mikaela felt a strange sense of pity for the man for whom the world must seem totally against. His eyes shifted to Mikaela, but he said nothing. For a moment there was complete silence over the group. It was as if time had stopped completely and all that existed were the crickets chirping in the grass and the magpies warbling in the distance.

Then Zac looked back at Thomas.

'Let me fly, Thomas. Let me get in the plane and fly away from here.'

'Not likely.'

'Look, I'm getting rid of my gun…' He slowly put his hand into his pocket and withdrew the gun gently, tossing the weapon away to his right where it landed on the ground. 'I'll taxi down to the back paddock and take-off. The police will find me, no doubt, but just give me one last fly in my plane.'

'Mikaela, get up here, away from that madman.'

Mikaela followed the cue, and stumbled up to the house to stand shakily beside Thomas. Now that she was close to him, the extent of his injuries was more apparent. One of his eyes was black and there was a nasty gash across the upper part of his forehead. The worst lesion appeared to be at his left shoulder, which had been heavily strapped with an old shirt. Even now fresh blood was beginning to seep through the material. She wondered how he was managing to keep his arm up to steady the shot-gun. She kept her distance in an effort to help his concentration. One unnecessary movement might cause him to stumble.

From some way off Mikaela could here sirens wailing. Zac must have heard them too, because his face turned white and his movements became edgy.

'I have to go, Thomas,' he said, moving towards the plane.

'Get back here or I'll shoot.'

'You won't shoot me now. You've got your woman back.' He opened the door of the plane.

'I'm warning you, Zac…'

'Let him go…' Mikaela found herself whispering, half to herself, half to her husband.

Thomas hesitated, then lowered the gun. They watched Zac start up the engine. The propeller began turning and buzzing, and in a moment the plane had turned and was bouncing slowly away from them, down to the flat part of the paddock. It picked up speed and then ran the length of the paddock before slowly lifting its nose upwards and climbing into the sky.

Mikaela felt her knees begin to shake.

'Is it over?' she whispered hoarsely.

Thomas was still watching the plane. The gun was now pointing at the ground, but his eyes remained fixed on the sky.

'He's not going to make it,' he muttered.

'What?' She followed his gaze to where the distant plane was still trying to gain altitude. It was climbing too slowly, and as she watched, it tried to clear the first group of tall gums that lined one of the roads further south. Mikaela opened her mouth to cry out but there was no sound, and she could only stare in horror as the wheels of the aircraft caught the top branches of the gums. In one sickening moment they saw the nose tip forward, and then the plane fell with a crash into the trees. In the next second, there was an explosion and a plume of black smoke began to rise from the burning wreckage.

'Oh Thomas, Thomas,' she heard herself repeating as she gazed at the smoke. She went to hold his arm, but his knees began to buckle underneath him and she tried to take his weight as he collapsed exhausted to the ground. She was dimly aware of sirens at the front of the house, doors slamming, men yelling. She put her head down against her lover's and gently rocked him.

Chapter Twenty

It was Thursday evening. Mikaela had cooked a roast for a belated birthday tea for Thomas, and her guests had all enjoyed the sumptuous meal, even if it was once again from a sheep. The room was filled with laughter and light, and Mikaela felt satisfied that she was able to entertain her friends in her own home.

Andy wiped the corner of his mouth with a serviette.

'Mikaela, you have excelled yourself. That was one of the best meals I have ever had.' He turned to the woman seated beside him. 'Are you taking notes?'

'Get real,' Erin said, her dark eyes shining. 'There'll only be bread and water for you, boy.'

'She loves me…' Andy grinned, and Erin slapped him with her serviette. Mikaela smiled at them both. It was so good to see Andy really happy at last.

Ian Scott took up the entire end of the table with his presence.

'How's the shoulder then?' he asked Thomas as he refilled

his glass.

'Not bad,' Thomas shrugged then winced. 'Except when I do that. The bone was shattered, so it will take a while to heal.'

Mikaela watched silently from the end of the table. The gash on Thomas' head was healing up nicely, even in just a few days. She couldn't believe he was still here to talk about things, when she found out what had happened…

It had of course been Zac's ute driving into the property that afternoon. The men had confronted each other, but Zac had the advantage of a weapon. There had been a struggle and then Zac had pulled the trigger, the shot firing into Thomas' shoulder. Thomas had hit the ground and passed out, and then woken up at the bottom of the cellar stairs.

'Could you send down the butter, Em?' David was helping himself to another slice of bread. 'I haven't quite worked out how you got out of the cellar, Thomas. Wasn't it locked?'

Thomas nodded.

'It was. But the old Winchester was still down there, so I ended up blasting the door handle off. I thought I'd been out to it for hours, but in reality it was probably only fifteen minutes or so.'

'And then you drove yourself to the Hamiltons?' Emily asked.

'No – I could hardly make it up the stairs. That's where Joey came in.'

The guests turned in unison towards the humble fishman who was seated down the table beside Elizabeth. He looked a little shy as he recounted his story.

'I was almost to the cellar when I heard this loud bang, and there's the door half off its hinges. I was a bit scared to go any further – thought he might blow me off me hinges too. But we sorted it out, and I got him up the stairs and out to the van. Then we drove over together.'

'But how did you know to go to the cellar?' Andy asked, chewing on an apple.

'That was Mrs McDowell's doing.'

Helen looked up suddenly and Joey stumbled on his words.

'I mean the younger one – I mean, not the younger one, the other one, umm...'

Helen smiled.

'It's alright, I know what you mean Joey. You mean Mikaela.'

'Yes, well, she and that Zac bloke looked pretty strange, standin' there like they was, and then she up and says to me she wants to order some fertilizer. Well, I mean, I don't sell fertilizer. I'm a fishman! I sell chicken.'

There was a general chuckle around the table.

'I thought it was a funny thing to say, and then suddenly I remembered I had helped Thomas shift a bag of fertilizer into the gardening room once, where the cellar is. So I figured she was trying to tell me to go back around to that room.'

'So you left in the van, but you came back.' This was from David.

'Yep. I drove out of the driveway, then down the road a few metres, then I cut round the back through the scrub and waited behind the trees till I knew it was all clear. Then I went back to check out what had happened.'

'If it wasn't for Joey turning up, I don't know if I would have made it out of there.' Thomas was shaking his head slowly.

'If your Mrs hadn't ordered those special cheeses for your party, I wouldn't have turned up at all.'

The table was silent for a moment.

'Saved by a cheese...' murmured Andy, sipping at his glass.

'Let's not think about all that,' Helen said brightly. 'The

main thing is that you're all here, you're all safe and we can celebrate Thomas' birthday together.'

'Here, here,' agreed Ian in a big voice. 'A toast to Thomas and his great family.'

'Cheers!' and glasses clinked and were downed.

'By the way, how is Mrs Hamilton?' Ian asked, finishing his drink.

'Recovering in Ballarat hospital,' Thomas replied. 'The police found her in the back of the chook pen. She must have run in there to hide – she was all beaten up.'

'It's like history repeating itself,' commented Emily. 'Apparently that's what Frederick Hamilton did to his wife. I believe that's how she died.'

Helen clicked her tongue and everyone shook their heads in disbelief.

'There is one more thing,' Thomas added, 'did Mikaela tell you that we found some interesting information in one of my old high school magazines? There was another McDowell, a year above me, good footballer. No relation as far as we know. He coached the younger kids.'

'Do you remember him at all?' Elizabeth asked.

'No, didn't even recognise his face in the pictures. But his name was Terence.'

'Terence…Thomas…' David seemed to be playing with the notion, 'Yes, I can see where Zac made the mistake.'

'I mean, we can only guess. We'll never really know…'

The room was quiet again, and Mikaela let her thoughts drift back to the moment when she saw the plane dipping into the trees. She hated what Zac had done to them all, but she still felt a great sense of sadness when she thought of the life he must have led. There had only been preliminary investigations, but already it had been discovered that Zac had been previously diagnosed with a psychiatric illness. There may have been a genetic link – Frederick Hamilton had demonstrated similar traits. His suicide had only worsened his son's state of mind, coupled with Zac's inability to say goodbye. There was no doubt that this poor soul had felt there was nowhere to turn in his manic life. The unspoken thought of course was whether the plane crash had been an accident at all...

Thomas' hand came over hers, bringing her back to the present. She looked across at him, and his eyes had locked onto hers.

'Come back, Mikaela girl,' he whispered. 'You were gone there for a moment.'

'Sorry. Everything's been so strange. Like a bad dream.'

'It's over now. It'll take time to work through, but we'll get there. We'll get there together.'

'I love you, Thomas McDowell.'

'I love you too.'

*****

Later they stood together at the gate of McDowell Hill, arms around each other, looking up at the dazzling sky above them. It was as if an unseen hand had scattered a million diamonds into the heavens.

'I remember when I first looked at the sky out here at night,' Mikaela murmured. 'We were on that car trial for the youth group.' She rested her head against Thomas' shoulder.

'I remember that night. It seems like a long time ago.' He stroked her hair gently with his fingertips.

'The stars are just as beautiful tonight as they were then. They haven't changed.'

'Some things never change.'

A cool breeze twirled around Mikaela's shoulders and she snuggled closer to her husband, enjoying the warmth of his body.

'We'll never change, will we Thomas? Our love for each

other, I mean.'

'Our love for each other will never change, Mikaela. There will be ups and downs, but we'll get through them. We'll learn from them.'

'And our God will never change. That's good to know too.'

She felt Thomas pull her closer and squeeze her arm.

'Yes, Mikaela. That is very good to know.'

They let the peace of the evening envelope them.

Chapter Twenty-One

The breeze was warm on Mikaela's face as she opened the door of the ute –summer would soon be upon them. The crops she had passed on either side of the road were looking glorious, acres and acres of golden healthy wheat. Harvest time was just around the corner, and it was promising to be a bumper yield – this had been one of the best years the farmers in the district had ever known. The children in Mikaela's class were counting down the days to the end of school when they could go out to help their parents bring in the crop.

Crickets chirped from the long grass around her shoes and magpies were warbling lazily from the gum trees above. It had been a long time since she had first come out onto the east road to the old hall. It still stood forlornly, paint peeling from the wooden walls, the dirty windows looking at her like sad eyes. She slowly wandered past the old stairs and peered up at the door. She had been inside the hall once before, but today she was not ready to journey into its past again. Today she was looking for something different.

She continued carefully towards the back of the hall, picking her way between the tall grass and fallen tree limbs, and keeping an eye out for snakes. Brown snakes were common in this part of the world, and especially at this time of year.

She stepped around to the rear and spied an ancient toilet block with crumbling brickwork and a gaping hole where the door should be. An old rusted tank lay disused amongst branches and leaves. Everything was so old and so forgotten. It made her feel sad that no-one ever used this place anymore.

A little further away from the toilet block was a group of old gums, creaking in the breeze like the bones of old women. Mikaela peered at the trees. As she drew nearer, she realised that there was a structure in amongst the trees - a corrugated iron shed. It had no door, just three walls and a roof that sloped back away from the doorway. Holding up the walls at the front corners were round pine posts, dusty and grubby with age but still showing the knots of wood. The inside of the shed was filled with tree branches and leaves. At one time the whole thing was probably quite stable – this morning it looked distinctly unstable.

'Is this the copper house?' Mikaela whispered into the air. She looked at the overgrown mess inside the shed. If it was, then this was where Bill would have sat, just inside the corner of the doorway, watching his grandmother at work. It would have been so different then – she imagined the evening, ladies and gentlemen from all over the district entering the hall for a social night of dancing, dressed in their best attire. The hall would have been lit up like a beacon in the countryside, and laughter and chatting would have poured from the open doors. Winter nights in the Mallee could be bitterly cold, so Bill would have sat here in the shed where it was warm, watching the fire flicker and his grandmother and great aunt heating up the water in the copper.

Mikaela patted the small torch in her jeans pocket and ventured carefully inside. The corrugated iron was warm where she placed her hand on the wall. A few galahs flew screeching in the air as she moved, making her jump, but once she had settled her breathing, she started to pull away some of the overgrowth that had invaded the shed. If this was the copper shed, there should be a copper. She moved carefully, noting large cobwebs in the corners of the roof, which probably housed even larger spiders. It was dim inside and she wished she had brought gardening gloves to protect her hands from the prickly scrub. Her feet crackled and crunched on the dead leaves, and little flying insects and moths spun away across the ground as she moved. Maybe the copper had been taken out long ago...

And then suddenly she pulled away a large branch and found an arrangement of bricks against the back wall, all crumbling and dirty with age, and sitting amongst the brickwork was a large black cast-iron mount. The structure almost reached her waist, and there was a rough wooden lid sitting across the top. She picked up the heavy lid and placed it carefully onto the ground, and then shone her torch down into the hole. A large round vessel filled the space, its metallic surface green and dark with time. Mikaela tapped inside with her knuckle and the vessel gave a dull ring.

She smiled and shook her head.

'Bill's copper,' she murmured. She ran her torch around the edges and down the sides, noting the bricked area under the base where the fire would have burned.

A magpie warbled again from a nearby tree, and Mikaela became conscious of the heat permeating the little shed and emanating from the iron walls. It would certainly be a warm little spot when the fire was lit and the copper was steaming. Her dry tongue longed for a sip of water from the bottle she had left in the ute, so she flashed her torchlight once more into the copper and was about to switch it off when something caught her eye. At the very bottom recess of the vessel there was something that wasn't metallic, a dark rectangular shape that was easy to miss in the dim grime of the copper. Mikaela reached her hand in, hoping there would be no crawly things waiting to spring upon her fingers, and withdrew a flat wooden box.

The box was dusty in her hands, leaving a brown stain on her fingertips. Switching off the torch, she made her way gingerly back outside, feeling her hands beginning to perspire not necessarily from the heat. In the broad daylight she stopped and had another look at the thing in her hands. The wood was dark and the box had a hinged lid. She shook her head, staring at it - what strange find was this then?

She wandered over to where a log was lying on the ground beside a tree and sat down gently, trying to calm herself. Placing the box on her knees, she carefully undid the latch and opened the lid.

Inside was a folded letter on slightly yellowed paper. She carefully took the letter out and saw that underneath lay a tarnished bangle. She pulled out the bangle with trembling fingers. It was black with age. Set into the bangle was a black stone, not unlike the one she wore on the pendant around her neck. She rubbed at it for a moment, feeling its coolness under her fingertips, then she slowly opened the letter. The handwriting was familiar immediately, and with a rapid heartbeat she began to read the words.

To my darling daughter,
I'm not sure if you will ever read this, and in some ways I hesitate to even write, knowing it may serve no purpose. I will send this package to Billy, with a covering note that he is to keep it safe for Lynny's daughter. Billy is the only one I

trust. If you ever go searching for your roots, perhaps your road will lead you to my Billy, and he will be able to pass this letter on to you.

I feel as if you have been gone forever and my heart has been ripped out. I did not want to give you away, but I knew that it would be the best for you. I named you Aislinn when you were born because it means 'dream', and that is all I have of you now, just a dream.

As for me, my life has changed forever. I exist now as somebody new. It is the only way I can move on in this world and escape all that has happened.

As for you, be brave in all circumstances and live life mightily. You will be in my thoughts forever.

With love on your first birthday,

Carolyn Farmer

July 22nd, 1979

The date swirled around in Mikaela's brain. 1979 – a year after she was born. The same Carolyn Farmer who had died during childbirth had written a letter and sent a parcel to Bill twelve months after her baby had been delivered.

Mikaela let her head drop back against the gum tree behind her. The significance of the letter began to seep slowly into her confused mind. Carolyn had not died during childbirth at all. She had given Mikaela up for adoption, and then disappeared into society.

Somehow Bill had hidden this treasure here in the copper during a visit to Turramore – perhaps he had come down for his father's or mother's funeral. Mikaela could gather more details from Elizabeth. But the incredible truth remained, blaringly obvious the more she thought about it - Carolyn Farmer could still be alive.

Mikaela closed her eyes against the sunshine. She let the letter drop to her lap and then rested her hand on her stomach where she knew a tiny new body was growing and forming in some secret place. She smiled and felt a peace come upon her. Whatever happened in the future, she knew that God's timing was perfect and she would trust Him to lead her along life's journey.

Carefully she replaced the letter and the bangle into the box.

It was time to go home.

The End

MOUNTAIN
Ash Road

Chapter One

I t's time to leave.

Mikaela shook the words from her mind as she watched the dirty brown water trickle pathetically from the hose. The silty liquid dribbled out onto the dry ground in front of her and the sun was hot on the back of her neck, unusually hot for the beginning of May.

She cast her eyes across the garden. The shrubs and vegetables she had planted six months ago were starting to shrivel away and the grass had died off and was beginning to resemble a worn grey carpet. She straightened her back as she looked out over the weary foliage, running one hand over the bulge at her stomach. It hadn't rained for months and now the dirty water from the hose meant that the dam was almost empty. No water meant no crops – no crops meant no money. And a baby would be born this year…

It's time to leave. The thought crept into her mind again like a cat and again she tried to push it away. How could she ever leave Turramore? The town was her lifeblood; the land

and the wheat around her had become her air. And Thomas would never leave. After so many years of hard toil he had built this homestead into what it was today. He had nurtured the soil and it had produced the best crops in the district. No, there was no way he would ever leave.

But crops are nothing without water, and water is not accessible unless it rains. Once again the fickle weather was having the last laugh. No amount of work could make up for lack of moisture in the earth.

She turned off the hose as a puff of dust blew into her face. The sky was reddening in the west – sunlight reflecting off more dust blown from the paddocks. One day the paddocks would blow away all together, leaving nothing to hold the seeds at cropping time. Maybe there wouldn't be a cropping time this year.

As she stepped up onto the verandah she heard the front gate screech and footsteps came up the concrete path beside the house. Thomas sauntered into view, pulling off his cap, his overalls dusty and his light brown hair dishevelled. He looked tired, but he smiled when he saw Mikaela and his blue eyes sparkled.

"How's my beautiful wife?"

"A bit grubby. I've been trying to water the garden, but there's nothing coming out of the hose."

Thomas shook his head.

"Dam's drying up. The whole place is drying up."

She watched him disappear into the laundry block to wash his hands and face. He reappeared drying his hands on a towel and squinting towards the sunset.

"I don't know, Mikaela. If we don't get rain soon, I'm not sure how productive the farm's going to be this year."

She nodded thoughtfully and together they were silent, gazing around at the house that was their home, listening to the sparrows chirping and the wind moving through

218

the peppercorn tree. Thomas slung the towel over his shoulder and came to stand beside Mikaela. Gently he placed his arm around her shoulders.

"I want to be able to provide for my family, for my children."

"I think there's only one in there, Thomas…"

"I know, but we are going to need money – there'll be hospital bills, clothes to buy…"

Mikaela nodded.

"I know. I've been thinking about it too."

She felt Thomas give a long sigh beside her.

"I'm wondering if I should get another job somewhere, just to bring in a bit extra."

Mikaela raised her eyes to look at him.

"We couldn't leave McDowell Hill."

"No, you wouldn't need to leave." He took her in his arms and looked into her eyes. "I could go away, just for a couple of months, earn some cash and then come home in time for the baby. You'd be fine here – Mum could come out and stay with you."

"A couple of months? Thomas, are you crazy? I couldn't be without you for a couple of months. I'd have to come too. We'd have to do it together."

"But you're – "

"Pregnant. I'm not sick, I don't have rabies, and my head hasn't fallen off. I'm just pregnant, and I'm still quite able to relocate and look after my husband." She drew him closer and wrapped her arms around his neck, enjoying his warmth.

"I don't want you to ever leave me, Thomas," she whispered in his ear. She leaned her head on his chest and they were silent for a while, watching the wind make little dust pools across the verandah.

"We'll figure something out," Thomas said finally. "We'll

pray about it."

Mikaela nodded and watched the setting sun. Yesterday she thought she would be at McDowell Hill forever. Today she wasn't so sure.

Tomorrow – what would tomorrow bring?

****

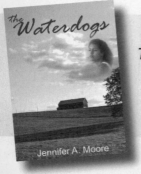

Change your life...

"Daniel's Diet is not just another diet book. This book is different. It's God's own diet drawn from His word."

Dr Cecile Lombard MD

Based on Daniel's diet from the book of Daniel— Naturopath & Nutritionist Philip Bridgeman has devised a 10-day detox and weight loss plan based on the scriptures, that actually works!

Daniel's Diet bridges the 2500-year gap between then and now.